ZAKHAR PRILEPIN

SIN

Glagoslav Publications

SIN
By Zakhar Prilepin

First published in Russian as "Грех"

Translated by Simon Patterson
together with Nina Chordas
Edited by Nina Chordas

Glagoslav Publications Ltd
88-90 Hatton Garden
EC1N 8PN London
United Kingdom

www.glagoslav.com

ISBN: 978-90-818239-3-7

Contents

Whatever day of the week it happens to be

My heart was absent. Happiness is weightless, and its bearers are weightless. But the heart is heavy. I had no heart. She had no heart either, we were both heartless.

Everything around us had become wonderful; and this "everything" sometimes seemed to expand, and sometimes froze, so that we could enjoy it. We did enjoy it. Nothing could touch us to the extent that it evoked any other reaction but a good, light laughter.

Sometimes she went away, and I waited. Unable to sit waiting for her at home, I reduced the time before our meeting and the distance between us, and went out into the yard.

There were puppies running around in the yard, four of them. We gave them names: Brovkin – a tough tramp with a cheerful nature; Yaponka – a slanty-eyed, cunning, reddish puppy; Belyak – a white runt, who was constantly trying to compete with Brovkin and always failing; and finally, Grenlan – the origin of her name was a mystery, and it seemed very suitable for this princess with sorrowful eyes, who piddled out of fear or adoration the minute anyone called her.

I sat on the grass surrounded by the puppies. Brovkin was lounging around on the ground not far away, and every time I called him, he energetically nodded to me. "Hello," he said. "It's great, isn't it?" Yaponka and Belyak fussed about, rubbing their noses in the grass. Grenlan was lying next to them. Every time I tried to pet her, she rolled on her back and squeaked: her entire appearance said that, although she had almost limitless trust in me, even revealing her pink belly, she was still so terrified, so terrified that she didn't have the strength to bear it. I was seriously worried that her heart would burst from fear. "Hey, what's wrong with you, darlin'!" I said to reassure her, looking with interest at her belly and everything that was arranged on it. "What a girl!"

I don't know how the puppies got into our courtyard. One time in the morning, incredibly happy even while asleep, calmly holding in my hands the heavy, ripe adornments of my darling, who was sleeping with her back to me, I heard the resonant sound of puppies barking – as if the little dogs had made the inexplicable things inside me material, and had clearly expressed my mood with their voices. Although, when I was first awakened by the puppies' noise, I was angry – they'd woken me up, and they could have woken up my Marysya too: but I soon realized that they were not barking just to bark, but were begging food from passers-by – I heard their voices too. They usually yelled at them to go away: "I don't have anything, get lost! Shoo! Get lost!"

I pulled on my jeans, that were lying around in the kitchen – we constantly got carried away and reeled around the apartment, until we were completely exhausted, and only in the morning, smiling rather foolishly, we traced our torrid paths by the pieces of furniture that we had displaced or knocked over, and by other inspired chaos – anyway, I pulled on my jeans and ran outside in the flip-flops which for some unknown reason I associated with my happiness, my love and my wonderful life.

The puppies, having failed to elicit any food from the succession of passers-by, tirelessly nosed around in the grass, digging up bits of rubbish, fighting over twigs and a piece of dry bone, time and again turning over an empty can – and naturally, this couldn't fill them up. I whistled, and they came running over to me – oh, if only my happiness would come running to me like this throughout my life, with this furious readiness. And they circled me, incessantly nuzzling against me, but also sniffing at my hands: bring us something to eat, man, they said with their joyful look.

"Right, folks!" I said and ran home.

I lunged at the fridge, opened it, knelt prayerfully before it. With my hand I tousled and stroked Marysya's white knickers, which I had picked up from the floor in the entry way, without of course being surprised as to how they had got there. The knickers were soft; the fridge was empty. Marysa and I were not gluttons – we just never really cooked anything, we had a lot of other things on our minds. We didn't want to be substantial like borshch, we fried large slabs of meat and immediately ate them, or, smearing and kissing each other, we whipped up egg-nog and drank that straight away too. There was nothing in the fridge, just an egg, like a viewer who had fallen asleep, in the cinema, surrounded by empty seats on both sides: above and below. I opened the freezer and was glad to discover a box of milk in it. With a crack, I ripped this box from its ancient resting-place, rushed to the kitchen and was happy once again to find flour. A jar of sunflower oil stood peacefully on the windowsill. *I'll make pancakes for you*!

Twenty minutes later I had made ten or so deformed specimens, raw in some places, burnt in others, but quite edible – I tried them myself and was satisfied. Jumping down two steps at a time, feeling in my hand the heat of the pancakes, which I had put in a plastic bag, I flew out of the building. While running down the stairs I worried that the puppies might have run away, but I was reassured as soon as I heard their voices.

"What wonderful pups you are!" I exclaimed. "Let's try the pancakes!"

Out of the bag I extricated the first pancake, which was balled up like all the rest. All four puppies opened their young, hot mouths at once. Brovkin – who got this name later – was the first to take a hot mouthful, pushing the others aside. It burned his mouth and he immediately dropped it, but he didn't leave it there, dragging it in several movements by half a meter into the grass, where he hurriedly bit it around the edges, then, shaking his head, swallowed it and came leaping back to me.

Waving the pancakes in the air to cool them down, I carefully gave each puppy a separate piece, though the mighty Brovkin managed to swallow both his own piece and to take pieces from his young relatives. However, he did this inoffensively, without humiliating anyone, as if he were fooling around. The puppy which we later called Grenlan got the fewest pancakes of all, and after a couple of minutes, when I'd learned to tell the puppies apart – they initially seemed indistinguishable – I started to shoo the pushy, fluffy-browed brothers and cunning red-furred sister away, so no one could snatch her sweet piece of pancake from this touching little creature, bashful even in her own family.

Thus, we became friends.

Every time I lied to myself shamelessly that a minute before my darling arrived, before she turned the corner, I could already sense her approach – something moved in the thickening blue air, somewhere an auto braked. I was already smiling like a fool, even when Marysya was still a long way off, thirty meters or so, and I couldn't stop smiling, and commanded the puppies: "Right then, let's meet my darling, quick! Do I feed you pancakes for nothing, you spongers!"

The puppies jumped up and, waggling their fluffy bodies, tripping from happiness, they ran to my darling, threatening to scratch her exquisite ankles. Marysenka stepped over them and comically shooed the puppies away with her little black purse. Everything inside me was trembling and twirling, like puppy tails. Still fending them off with her purse, Marysenka wandered over to me, sat down with flawless elegance, and inclined her cool, fragrant, pebble-smooth neck, so that I could kiss it. In the instant that I kissed her, she moved away by a fraction of a millimeter, or rather shuddered – of course, I hadn't shaved. I hadn't found the time to do so all day – I was busy: I was waiting for her. I couldn't take my mind off her. Marysya took one of the puppies with both hands and looked it over, laughing. The puppy's belly showed pink, and three hairs stuck out, sometimes with a tiny white drop hanging from them.

"Their mouths smell of grass," Marysya said and added in a whisper: "green grass."

We left the puppies to play together, and went to the shop, where we bought cheap treats, annoying the saleswomen with the huge amount of spare change that Marysya dug out of her bag, and I took out of my jeans. Often, the irritated saleswomen didn't even count the change, but disdainfully scooped it up and poured it into the angular cavity of the cash register, not the section for the copper coins, but the "white" coins – the ones worth one kopeck and five kopecks, which had completely lost any purchasing power in our country, as it cheerfully slid into poverty. We laughed, no one's disdainful irritation could belittle us.

"Notice how today doesn't seem like a Tuesday," Marysya observed as we left the shop. "Today feels like Friday. On Tuesdays, there are far fewer children outdoors, the girls aren't dressed so brightly, the students are busier and the cars aren't so slow. Today time has definitely shifted. Tuesday has turned into Friday. What will tomorrow be, I wonder?"

I was amused at her intentionally bookish language – this was one of the things we did for fun, to talk like this. Later our speech became ordinary human speech – incorrect constructions, interjections, hints and laughter. None of this can be reproduced – because every phrase had a story behind it, every joke was so charming and fundamentally stupid that another repetition would kill it dead, as though it was born a fragile flower that immediately started to wilt. We spoke in the normal language of people who are in love and happy. They don't write like that in books. I can only single out a few individual phrases. For example this one:

"I visited Valies," Marysya said. "He proposed that I get married."

"To him?"

What a stupid question. Who else?

...The actor Konstantin Lvovich Valies was an old, burly man with a heavy heart. His heart was probably no longer beating, but rather sinking.

His mournful Jewish eyes under heavy, caterpillar-like eyelids had completely lost their natural cunning. With me, as with a youth, he still kept his poise – he was bitterly ironic, as it seemed to him, and frowned patronizingly. With her, he could not conceal his vulnerability, and this vulnerability appeared as a bare white stomach under a badly tucked-in shirt.

Once, as someone who does anything to earn money as long it's legal, including writing the stupid rubbish which usually serves to fill up newspapers, I asked Valies for an interview.

He invited me to his home.

I arrived a little earlier, and blissfully smoked on a bench by the house. I rose from the bench and went to the entranceway. Glancing at my watch, and seeing that I had another five minutes, I went back to the swings that I had just walked past, and touched them with my fingers, feeling the cold and roughness of the rusty iron bars. I sat on a swing and pushed off gently with my legs. The swing gave a light creaking noise. It seemed familiar to me, reminding me of something. I rocked on the swing again and heard quite clearly: *V-va... li... es...* I rocked on the swing again. "Va-li-es" – the swing creaked. *Va-li-es.* I smiled and jumped off rather clumsily – at my back, the swing shrieked out something with an iron hiss, but I couldn't tell what it was. The door of the entranceway muttered something in the same tone as the swing.

I forgot to say that Valies was a senior actor at the Comedy Theater in our town; otherwise there would have been no reason for me to visit him. No one asked me who I was through the door when I knocked – in the best of Soviet traditions, the door opened wide, and Konstantin Lvovich smiled.

"Are you the journalist? Come in..."

He was short and thick-set, his abundantly wrinkled neck showed his age, but his impeccable actor's voice still sounded rich and important.

Valies smoked, shaking off the ash with a swift movement, gesticulated, raised his eyebrows and kept them there just a tad longer than an ordinary person, who was no artist, could. But this all suited Konstantin Lvovich – the raised eyebrows, the glances, the pauses. As he talked, he deployed all of this skillfully and attractively. Like chess, in a definite order. And even his cough was artistic.

"Excuse me," he always said when he coughed, and where the sound of the last syllable of "Excuse me" ended, the next phrase would immediately continue.

"So then… Zakhar, right? So then, Zakhar…" – he would say, carefully pronouncing my somewhat rare name, as if he were tasting it with his tongue, like a berry or a nut.

"Valies studied at the theatrical academy with Yevgeny Yevstigneev, they were friends!" I repeated to Marysenka that evening what Konstantin Lvovich himself had said to me. Yevstigneev in a dark little room with a portrait of Charlie Chaplin by his squashed bed – the young and already bald Yevstigneev, living with his mother who quietly fussed behind the plywood wall, and Valies paying him a visit, curly-haired, with bright Jewish eyes… I imagined all this vividly to myself – and in rich colors, as if I had seen it myself, I described it to my darling. I wanted to surprise her, I liked surprising her. And she enjoyed being surprised.

"Valies and Yevstigneev were the stars of their year, they were such a cheerful pair, two clowns, one with curly hair and the other bald, a Jew and a Russian, almost like Ilf and Petrov. Just fancy that…" I said to Marysya, looking into her laughing eyes.

"What happened after that?" Marysya asked.

After he graduated from the academy, Zhenya Yevstigneev wasn't accepted into our Comedy Theater – they said that they didn't need him. But Valies was accepted immediately. Also, he started to appear in films, at the same time as Yevstigneev, who moved to Moscow. In the space of a few years, Valies played the poet Alexander Pushkin three times and the revolutionary Yakov Sverdlov three times as well. The films were shown all over the country… Valies also played a harmless Jew in a war film, together with Shura Demyanenko, who was famous at the time. And then he played Judas in a film where Vladimir Vysotsky played Christ. Although, truth to say, work on this film was stopped before shooting ended. But on the whole, Valies' acting career got off to a very lively start.

"…But then they stopped putting Valies into films," I said to Marysya.

He waited for an invitation to appear in another film, but it never came. So he didn't become a star, although in our town, of course, he was almost considered one. But theater productions came and went and were forgotten, and his obscure films were also forgotten, and Valies got old.

In conversation, Valies was ill-tempered, and swore. It was good that way. It would have been very sad to look at an old man with a sinking heart… The smoke dispersed, and he lit another cigarette – with a match, for some reason, there was no lighter on the table.

His time was passing, and was almost gone. Somewhere, once, in some distant day, he had been unable to latch on, to grasp something with his tenacious youthful fingers that would enable him to crawl out into that space bathed in warm, beery sunshine, where everyone is granted fame during their lifetime and promised love beyond the grave – perhaps not eternal love, but such that you won't be forgotten at least for the duration of a memorial drinking party.

Valies crushed the next cigarette into the ash tray, waved his hands, and the yellow tips of his fingers flashed by – he smoked a lot. He held in the smoke, and as he slowly exhaled, he became lost in the smoke, not squinting his eyes, throwing his head back. It was clear that everything was fading away, and now the whites of eyes were shining amid the pink veins, and his big lips were moving, and his heavy eyelids were trembling....

"Do you feel sorry for him, Marysenka?"

The next day I typed up the interview, read it over and took it to Valies. I handed it over and scurried off. Valies saw me off tenderly. And rang me up as soon as I was barely home. Perhaps he had started ringing earlier – the call arrested me just as I entered the apartment. The actor's voice was trembling. He was extremely angry.

"The interview can't appear in this form!" he almost shrieked.

I was somewhat taken aback.

"All right then, it won't," I said as calmly as possible.

"Goodbye!" he said curtly, and slammed the receiver.

"What did I do wrong?" I wondered.

Every morning, we were woken by barking – the puppies continued to beg for food from passers-by on their way to work. The passers-by cursed them – the puppies dirtied their clothes with their paws.

But once on a deep morning that merged into noon, I did not hear the puppies. I felt anxious while I was still asleep: something was obviously lacking in the languid confusion of sounds and reflections that precede awakening. An emptiness arose, it was like a funnel that was sucking away my sleepy peace.

"Marysenka! I can't hear the puppies!" I said quietly, and with such horror as if I couldn't find the pulse on my wrist.

Marysenka was terrified herself.

"Quick, run outside!" she also whispered.

A few seconds later, I was jumping down the steps, thinking feverishly: *Did a car run them over? What, all four of them? That can't be...* I ran into the sun and into the scent of warmed earth and grass, and the quiet noises of a car around the corner, and whistled, and shouted, repeating the names of the puppies one after another and then at random. I circled the untidy yard, overgrown with bushes. I looked under each bush – but didn't find anyone there.

I ran around our incredible building, incredible because on one side it had three stories, and on the other it had four. It was situated on a slope, and so the architects decided to make the building multi-levelled – so that the roof would be even; the building could easily drive insane an alcoholic who was attempting to judge how far off he was from the D.T.s by counting the number of stories in this decrepit but still mighty "Stalin-era" building.

I thought about this briefly again as I walked around the building slowly, banging on the water pipes for some reason, and looking into the windows. There were no puppies, nor any traces of them.

Terribly upset, I returned home. Marysya immediately understood everything, but still asked:

"No?"

"No."

"I heard someone calling them in the morning," she said. "That's right, I did. It was some guy with a hoarse voice."

I looked at Marysya, my whole appearance demanding that she remember what he said, this guy, and how he talked – I would go and find him in the town by his voice, and ask him where my puppies were.

"The tramps probably took them," Marysya said resignedly.

"What tramps?"

"A whole family of them lives not far from here, in a Khrushchev-era building. A few men and a woman. They often walk back past our home with [rubbish bags]. They probably lured the puppies to go with them.

"Do you mean… they could eat them?"

"They eat anything."

For a moment I pictured this all to myself – how my jolly friends were lured by deceit and thrown in a bag. How they squealed as they were carried. How happy they were when they were dumped out of the bag in the apartment – and at first the puppies even liked it: the delicious smell of tasty, rotting meat and… what's that other smell? Stale alcohol…

Perhaps the tramps even played with the puppies a little – after all, they're people too. They may have stroked their backs and tickled their tummies. But then came dinner time… *They couldn't have butchered them all at once?* I thought, almost crying. *Maybe two... maybe three.* I imagined these agonizing pictures, and I even started shaking.

"Where do they live?" I asked Marysenka.

"I don't know."

"Who does?"

"Maybe the neighbors do?"

Silently I put my shoes on, thinking what weapon to take with me. There wasn't any weapon in the house apart from a kitchen knife, but I didn't take it. *If I stab a tramp or all the tramps with this knife, then I'll have to throw it away,* I thought gloomily. I went around the neighbors' apartments, but most of them had already gone to work, and those who were at home were mainly elderly, and couldn't understand what I wanted from them – something about puppies, something about tramps... Besides, they didn't open their doors to me. I got sick of explaining things to the peepholes of wooden doors which I could knock down with three or so kicks. After calling one of the neighbors an "old moron," I ran out of our building, and headed to the building where the tramps lived.

I reached the Khrushchev-era building, almost running, and as I approached it I tried to determine which was the ill-fated tramps' den by looking at the windows. I couldn't work it out; there were too many poor and dirty windows, and only two that were clean. I ran into the building and rang the doorbell of apartment №1.

"Where do the tramps live?" I asked.

"We're tramps ourselves," a man in his underpants replied sullenly, looking me over. "What do you want?"

I looked over his shoulder, foolishly hoping that Brovkin would jump out to meet me. Or the pitiful Grenlan would crawl out, dragging intestines behind her. The apartment was dark, and there was a bicycle in the entry. Twisted and dirty door-mats lay on the floor. The door to apartment №2 was opened by a woman from the Caucasus, and several swarthy kids came running out. I didn't bother explaining anything to them, although the woman immediately started talking a lot. I didn't understand what she was talking about. I went up to the second floor.

"There's an apartment with tramps living in it in your building," I explained to a tidy-looking old woman, who was coming down the stairs. "They robbed me, and I'm looking for them."

The old woman told me that the tramps lived in the next entranceway on the second floor.

"What did they steal?" she asked, as I was already going down the stairs.

"My bride," I was going to joke, but I thought better of it.

"This one thing…"

I looked around outside – perhaps there was some blunt instrument I could take. There wasn't any to be found, or I would have taken one. I didn't try to break a branch off the American maple tree growing in the yard – you couldn't break it if you tried, you could spend a whole week bending the soft, fragile branch, and it wouldn't do any good. It's a wretched, ugly tree, I thought vengefully and angrily, somehow linking the tramps with American maples and America itself, as if the tramps had been brought over from there. The second floor –

where should I go? This door, probably. The one that looks the worst. As if people had been pissing on it for several years. And it's splintered at the bottom, revealing the yellow wood.

I pressed the door bell, stupidly. Yes, that's right, it will ring out with a trill, just press it harder. For some reason I wiped my finger on my trousers, having touched a doorbell that had been silent for one hundred years, and didn't even have wires attached to it. I listened to the noises behind the door, hoping of course to hear the puppies.

Have you already devoured them, you skunks?... I'll show you…

For an instant I contemplated what to hit the door with – my fist or my foot. I even raised my foot, but then hit it with my fist, not very hard, and then harder. The door opened with a hiss and a creak, just by a crack. I pushed the door with my hands – it dragged across the floor, over a worn track. I stepped into semi-darkness and a nauseating smell, firing myself up with a bitterness that simply wilted from the stench.

"Hey!" I called, willing my voice to sound rough and harsh, but the call came out stifled.

What should I call them? 'Hey, people', 'Hey, tramps'? They're not actually tramps, if they have a place of residence.

I examined the floor, for some reason convinced that I would put my foot into slimy filth if I took another step. I took a step. The floor was firm. The kitchen was to the left, and to the right was a room. I felt sick. I let a long line of spit, the precursor to vomit, out of my mouth. The line of spit swayed, fell and hung on the wall that was covered with wallpaper that was ripped in the form of a peak.

Why is the wallpaper in these apartments always ripped? Do they rip it on purpose or something?

"What are you spitting for?" a hoarse voice asked. "You're in a house, you fuck."

I couldn't tell at first whether the voice was a man's or a woman's. And where was it coming from – the room, or the kitchen? I wasn't visible from the room, so it must be from the kitchen. It was also dark in the kitchen. As I looked in, I realized that the windows were covered with sheets of plywood. I took another step towards the kitchen, and saw a person sitting at the table.The sex of the person was still unclear. A lot of disheveled hair… Barefoot… Pants, or something like pants, which ended above the knees. It seemed that there was a wound on the person's bare leg. And something was writhing in the wound, in a large quantity. Maybe I just imagined it in the dark.

There were a lot of bottles and cans on the table.

We were silent. The person wheezed, not looking at me. Suddenly, the person coughed, the table shook and the bottles chimed. The person coughed with all his insides, his lungs, bronchi, kidneys, stomach, nose, every pore. Everything inside him rumbled and seethed, spraying mucus, spit and bile around him. The sour air in the apartment slowly moved and thickened around me. I realized that if I took a single deep breath, I would catch several incurable diseases, which would in short order make me a complete invalid with pus-filled eyes and uncontrollable bloody diarrhea.

I stood to attention, without breathing, in front of the coughing tramp, as if he were a general giving me a dressing-down. The coughing gradually died down, and in conclusion, the tramp spat out a long trail of spit on to the floor, and wiped his mouth with his sleeve. Finally, I decided to go into the kitchen.

"I've come for the puppies!" I said loudly, almost choking, because as I opened my mouth, I did not breathe. My words sounded wooden. "Hey you, where are the puppies?" I asked with a last gasp: it was as if my shoulder had hit a pile of wood and several logs had rolled off it, dully thumping to the ground.

The person looked up at me and coughed again. I almost ran into the kitchen, scared that I would fall unconscious and would lie here, on the floor, and these vermin would think that I was one of them, and put me to lie with them. Marysenka would come and see me lying next to tramps. I kicked the bare legs of the tramp, that were in my way, and it looked as if several dozen little midges flew up off the wound on his ankle.

"Damn it!" I cursed, breathing heavily, no longer able to hold my breath. The person I had kicked swayed and fell over, taking the bottles on the table with him, and they fell on him, and the chair that he was sitting on also fell over, with two legs stuck in the air. And they were not positioned diagonally, but on the same side. *It couldn't stand up! You can't sit on it!* I thought, and shouted:

"Where are the puppies, scum?!"

The person squirmed about on the floor. Something trickled under my shoes. I tore the plywood board from the window, and saw that the window was partially smashed, and so this was evidently why it had been covered over. In the window, between the partitions, there was a half-liter bottle containing a solitary limp pickle covered in a white beard of mold that Father Christmas could have envied.

"Damn it! Damn!" I cursed again, helplessly looking over the empty kitchen, in which several broken crates were lying around in addition to the upside-down chair. There was no gas stove. A tap was leaking in the corner. In the sink lay a mound of half-rotten vegetables. All kinds of creatures with feelers or wings were crawling over the vegetables.

I jumped over the person lying on the floor and raced into the room, almost falling over the clothes piled on the floor – coats, jackets, rags. Perhaps someone was lying under the rags, huddled there. The room was empty, there was just an old television in the corner, with the picture tube intact. The window was also covered over with plywood boards.

"Who do you think you are!" the voice shouted to me from the kitchen. "I'm a boxer, asshole."

"Where are the puppies, boxer-asshole?" I mocked him, but didn't go back to the kitchen. Instead, overcoming my squeamishness, I opened the door to the toilet. There was no toilet bowl: just a gaping hole in the floor. In the bath, as yellow as lemonade, there were shards of glass and empty bottles.

"What puppies?" the voice shouted again, and added several dozen incomprehensible noises resembling either complaining or swearing.

The voice definitely belonged to a man.

"Did you take the puppies?" I shouted at him, leaving the toilet and looking for something in the corridor to hit him with. For some reason I thought there should be a crutch here, I thought I had seen one.

"Did you eat the puppies? Talk! Did you eat the puppies, you cannibals?" I screamed.

"You ate them yourself!" he shouted in reply.

I picked up a long-collapsed coat rack from the floor, threw it at the man lying in the kitchen and began to look for the crutch again.

"Sasha!" the tramp called to someone. He was still squirming, unable to stand up.

"Crack!" the bottle he threw at me clanked against the wall.

"Thief!" sobbed the man writhing on the floor, looking for something else to throw at me.

He had obviously cut himself on something – blood was streaming profusely from his hand.

He threw an iron mug at me, and another bottle. I managed to avoid the mug, and comically kicked the bottle away.

OK, that's enough... I thought and ran out of the apartment. In the entryway I checked to make sure that there was no slimy mud on me. It didn't look like it. The air hit me from all sides – how wonderful and clean the air is in entryways, my God. A trail of murky and sour filth, almost visible, crawled towards me from the tramps' den – and I ran down to the first floor, madly smiling about something.

I could hear shouts still coming from the apartment on the second floor.

"They were also children once," Marysya said to me back home. "Imagine how they ran around with their pink bellies..."

"They were," I replied without thinking, not having firmly decided whether they were or not. I tried to remember the face of the man in the kitchen, but couldn't.

When I got home I got into the bath and scrubbed myself with a sponge for a long time, until my shoulders turned pink.

"They couldn't have eaten them in one morning? They couldn't, could they?" Marysenka asked me loudly from behind the door.

"No, they couldn't!" I replied.

"Perhaps they were taken away by other tramps?" Marysya suggested.

"But they should have squealed," I thought out loud. "Wouldn't they have whined when they were thrown into the sack? We would have heard them."

Marysenka fell silent, evidently thinking to herself.

"Why are you taking so long? Come to me!" she called, and by her voice I understood that she hadn't reached any definite conclusion about the puppies' fate.

"You come to me," I replied.

I stood up in the bath, scattering foam from my hands on to the floor, and reached for the latch. Marysya stood by the door and looked at me with merry eyes.

For an hour we forgot about the puppies. I thought with surprise that we had been together for seven months, and every time – and we had probably done this several hundred times now – every time it was better than the last. Although the last time it seemed that it couldn't be better.

What can this be? I thought, moving my hand across her back, which incredibly narrowed at the waist and merged into a white magnificence, just left by me. It was covered with pink spots, I had rumpled it so thoroughly.

My hand became limp, although a minute ago it had been firm, and had tenaciously, painfully clutched the cheekbones of my darling's face – when I was behind her, I loved looking at her – and I turned her face towards me: to see what was there in her eyes, to look at her lips…

We were coming back from the shop almost two weeks later – we had probably buried them in our minds during this time, although we didn't talk about it out loud – and they reappeared. The puppies, as though nothing had happened, flew out to meet us and immediately scratched up the beautiful legs of my darling and left traces of their cheerful paws on my beige jeans.

"Guys! You're alive!" I shouted, lifting them all up in turn and looking into the puppies' foolish eyes.

Last of all, I tried to take Grenlan into my arms, but as usual she immediately rolled on to her back, revealing her stomach, and puffed herself up either out of fear or happiness, or out of endless respect for us.

"Give them something!" Marysenka ordered.

I couldn't give them raw, frozen dumplings, and so I opened the yoghurt, pouring the pink substance right on to the crumpled asphalt. They licked it all up and started running around us in circles, around Marysya and me, and every time they circled they rubbed their noses in the dark marks left by the yoghurt that had instantly vanished.

"Give them some more!" Marysya said, smiling with her eyes.

We fed the puppies four yoghurts and went home happily, talking about where the puppies had vanished for so long. We didn't work it out, of course.

The puppies settled into our yard again.

Summer came to a full boil outside, steaming and trembling, and when we opened the window in the morning, we could call out to the puppies, who ran around in circles, unsure who was calling them, but very happy about the chicken bones that fell from the sky.

The days were important – every day. Nothing happened, but everything was very important. The lightness and weightlessness were so important and full that you could whip up enormous, heavy featherbeds out of them. Lively yelping could be heard outside the window every day.

"Maybe they were killed, suffocated, drowned… and they returned from the other world? So we wouldn't be distressed?" Marysenka said one night.

Her voice seemed to ring softly like a bell, and the words were so tangible that if you squinted in the darkness, you could probably see them fluttering, and falling lightly, swaying in the air.

And the next day you could find them on books, or under the bed, or somewhere else – to the touch, they would probably resemble the wings of a dried-up insect, which would disintegrate as soon as you picked them up.

"Can you imagine?" she asked. "They came back to life, that's it. Because we can't be distressed this summer. Because one like this is never going to happen again."

I didn't want to talk about it. And I reminded her how Belyak constantly tried to conquer Brovkin, and how Brovkin would easily knock him over, and run off, indifferent toward the conquered puppy, and would lie on the grass once more, majestically, like a lion cub, regarding his surroundings. And also, in a hurry to speak, I recalled Yaponka, her cunning fox-like eyes and unfathomable nature. Marysenka was silent.

Then I started talking about Grenlan, about how she piddled out of fear or happiness, although my darling knew about all of this and had seen it for herself, but she joined in with my stories, adding her tenderness and her carefree laughter – first one small colorful ribbon, then another, barely noticeable. And I kept talking, not even talking, but weaving… or paddling – paddling even faster with the oars, taking my darling away in a fragile boat… or perhaps not paddling, but pedaling, taking her away on a bicycle frame, pressed against me with her hot skin… in general, leaving behind all the things you return to, no matter what you do.

"Listen, we don't have much money. We can earn some. The newspaper editor said that he wanted an interview with Valies. But I don't have an interview."

"But you did interview him?" Marysya looked at me.

"I told you that he..."

"Yes, yes, I remember... So what can we do? If we had some money, we could go out. We need money to go out. To get out of the house."

We thought in silence.

"Ring Valies. Ask him: 'What didn't you like?'"

"No, I won't do that. He'll yell at me."

"What didn't he like?"

"I portrayed him as an angry person. A violator of the peace, of order... But he was just gossiping. Nasty old man."

"What's with you? Why are you talking like that?"

"He's a nasty old man! He called everyone names, but won't let me print it. What's he go to lose? Just imagine the scandal!"

"You should just print it without asking."

"No, that's not right... Nasty old man."

We fell silent again. I poured Marysenka some tea. Steam rose from the cup.

"Listen," I said. "Why don't you interview him?"

"I can't. How do you interview someone? I'm afraid."

"What are you afraid of? I'll write you a list of questions. You'll go and read them. And he'll reply. Turn on the Dictaphone, and that's it. And we'll get some money."

I was happy with this unexpected idea, and excitedly I began trying to convince Marysenka that she had to go visit Valies and interview him. And I persuaded her in the end.

She spent a long time preparing. She found some old brochure about Valies, and learnt it all by heart, and tirelessly repeated the questions I had written out for her, as if she were getting ready for an exam.

"What if he tells me to get lost?" Marysenka kept asking. "I don't understand anything about the theater."

"What do you mean? Unlike me you've actually been to one."

"No, I don't understand anything."

"But journalists don't understand anything at all. It's accepted. And they write about everything. That's the main thing in journalism – to have absolutely no idea about anything and express your opinions about everything."

"No, that's not right. Perhaps we should go to a few plays first?"

"Marysenka, you must be mad, that won't pay off. Go to Valies right now. Go on, ring him now, before he dies, he's an old man."

"Listen, you stop it. I've got to get ready."

She didn't ring him until the next day, and made me go into the other room, so that I wouldn't hear or see her talking on the phone, and wouldn't make silly faces at her.

Valies agreed with dignity – Marysya told me how he replied to her on the phone, and together we reached the conclusion that he was agreeing "with dignity." I saw her to Valies' house and waited for her to return.

I imagined them sitting there, and him smoking… Or wasn't he smoking? I couldn't imagine anything further: I kept getting distracted by the thought of Marysya sitting in the chair, in her dark pants, and how when she reached for the Dictaphone that was sitting on the table, to turn the cassette over, her sweater would hike up a little, baring her back, and a scrap of her knickers could be visible, just a bit at the waistband… I didn't have the strength to think any more, and went for a walk.

I walked around the building, and gawked at the children – there were a lot fewer of them in town compared with my childhood, which seemed to have ended not so long ago. After I counted the corners of the building, I squatted under a slanted roof, smoked the last cigarette in the packet, and decided to give up smoking. Although "decided" isn't quite the right word: I fully understood that I wouldn't smoke any more – because cigarettes were not at all in keeping with my mood, smoking was a completely superfluous, unnecessary, time-wasting activity.

Why do I smoke, if I'm so happy? I thought, and again, for the umpteenth time, I caught myself smiling – without realizing it. And this made me smile even more happily, and imagining how foolish I must look, I laughed out loud.

Marysenka returned one and a half hours later. I had almost started smoking again in that time.

"How was he then?" I asked her.

"He was fine," Marysenka said smiling.

"What did you talk about?"

"I don't remember…" The smile didn't leave her face.

"What do you mean, you don't remember? You just said goodbye, didn't you?"

"Can you imagine, I lost the piece of paper with your questions on it, and forgot everything immediately."

"How did you do it then?"

"I don't even know... We'll listen to the Dictaphone when we get home... I want an apple. Buy me an apple..."

I bought her an apple, from an old woman with a basket of them.

"It's worm-eaten," Marysenska said after taking a few bites.

"Throw it away," I ordered.

"If it's worm-eaten, that means it's real," she replied.

We walked four stops, holding each other by the arm. We scraped up enough money for a bottle of cheap wine and drank it by the kiosk, like alcoholics. There was a smell of urine. We kissed until we reached a state of indecent exhaustion that threatened to lead to acts of folly – on a street that was still full of cars, though already getting dark. Then we would calm down for a few minutes.

"How are we going to live?" Marysenka asked, smiling.

"Wonderfully."

"Will there be a plot?"

"A plot? A plot is when everything runs dry. But for us it keeps on flowing and flowing."

We quietly walked home, but we had to go up a hill, and Marysya started complaining that she was tired. I settled her on my shoulders. Marysenka sang a song, she loved riding horseback. I also liked carrying her, I held Marysya by the ankles and wiggled my head, trying to find a position so that my neck was warm and even a little damp.

A day later Marysya went to Valies to verify the interview. We had made the interview good-natured and calm, and as a result it turned out rather dull. Marysya was satisfied when she came back from Valies: he liked the interview, and he was full of praise for Marysenka, but he suggested several additions to the text, and so asked her to come back again. When exactly he didn't say, but he promised to call.

"Couldn't he have made those additions right away?" I said, laughing.

"He's probably unhappy. He doesn't have a wife. He lives alone," Marysenka explained. "He says that he's very lonely."

"Does he smoke in your presence?" I asked for some reason.

"No, he doesn't. He says that he gave it up."

Fancy that, he 'gave it up', I thought with ironic anger. *Why doesn't he smoke? I wonder.... I don't smoke because I'm happy, what's his reason?*

"Well, how was he with you?" I asked, secretly feeling an affinity with Valies, because he evoked these fine emotions in my darling.

"You know, everyone's so funny... These old men... Valies... He once also had a mother, after all, he was also a child. Like all of us. And we all behave how we were once taught: mothers... then kindergarten... So everything is very similar, very simple. Do you understand me?"

I thought that I understood very well. Valies had a mother. Marysya had a mother. So did I. What was not to understand about that?

I was sitting with the puppies in the yard, waiting for Marysenka. She arrived and we all cheered up.

"I went to visit Valies," Marysenka said. "He made me a marriage proposal."

"To marry whom?"

I laughed myself at my stupid question. Marysenka laughed too.

"Can you imagine?" she related, "He rang me, and sounded so prim. '*…Might you be able to pay me a visit today…*'"

"For the additions to the interview?"

Marysenka laughed again.

"Just imagine, I went to his apartment, and he opened the door – wearing a coat and tails. Like a candelabrum… Black and ceremonial. And he smelt of eau de cologne. I looked into the apartment – and a huge table was laid: candles, wine, dishes. What a nightmare!"

"And then what happened?"

"I didn't even take my things off. I lied to him…" Marysenka looked at me with happy eyes. "I told him that I had a small child. That he was home alone."

"Was he stunned?"

"No, he generally behaved very decently. He didn't make any fuss. He said: 'Well, never mind, next time…' Then he said that he was preparing a play... 'About the love of an old, wise man for a young woman' – that's what he said... And he offered the leading role to me."

"The old, wise man?"

We laughed again. And our laughter did not degrade Valies in any way. If anyone else who was keeping track of all the evil on earth had heard our laughter, he would probably have confirmed this – because we were simply happy that we had met Valies, that he wore a coat and tails, and that he was so nice... "An old, wise man." And the young women in the leading role was next to me. And I was there..

"And then he proposed to me to marry him," Marysenka concluded.

I didn't ask what that was like. I simply looked at Marysenka.

"What could I do?",she replied, as if in justification, to my questioning look. "I said: 'Konstantin Lvovich, you are a very good man. Can I ring you again?' He said: 'Definitely call...' And that was all, I ran off. I didn't even wait for the lift..."

"He's probably sitting there by himself," I said, unexpectedly becoming sad. "Marysya... You could have drunk a bottle with him... Aren't you sorry for him?"

"What? No, I can't do that. I couldn't. That would be wrong. What are you saying? He asked me to marry him, and I'm supposed to eat herring salad."

"He had herring salad?" I asked with interest.

We laughed again, patting the puppies that were hanging around at our feet.

"I'm hungry," said Marysenka.

"You should have eaten when you were at Valies' place," I couldn't resist joking. "Shall we visit him together? You can say: 'this is your old acquaintance. He's come to apologize. And he also wants to act in the play'…"

"The role of a young, stupid man…" Marysenka continued.

"We'll sit at the table, talk and drink. We'll discuss the upcoming play. OK? What else did he have on the table? Besides herring…"

"There wasn't any herring there.

"But you said…"

We were very hungry. Almost weightless from hunger.

"Why don't we go out? I really do feel like herring. And vodka with tomato juice. Is it terrible that I feel like vodka?"

"What do you mean? It's glorious."

Valies started ringing almost every day. Sometimes I answered the phone, and he, not recognizing me and not at all abashed that a man had answered, he asked to speak with her, calling my darling by her first name and patronymic. He even invited her to his birthday party, either his sixty-ninth or his seventy-first , but she didn't go. Valies wasn't offended, he rang again, and sometimes they talked for a long time. Marysya listened, and he talked to her. *Perhaps he's saying improper things to her,* I thought the first time, but Marysenka was so serious and asked him such questions that I soon forgot these stupid ideas.

"He told me that they're not letting put on the play. That they're insulting him. He has no one to talk to," said Marysenka. "He says that I understand him".

Valies became part of our conversations over tea, and also without tea.

"How's Konstantin Lvovich doing?" I would often ask.

Marysenka smiled thoughtfully, and did not let me make jokes about the old man. I didn't even want to.

I had someone to make jokes about and someone to adore. Brovkin grew into a broad-chested guy with a fine voice. We played well together – on the rare occasions when I came home drunk, he brought me a stick, and we played tug-of-war. He always won.

He was the first to be taken away – the neighbors said that they needed a smart and strong guard in their garage. Brovkin was very suitable for them, I knew. The neighbors also took Yaponka for their friends – she was considerably larger than the small Belyak, and so they took the girl. And Belyak was taken away at the end of summer by a guy in a truck. He stuck his head out the window in a half-unbuttoned shirt, sunburnt, smiling, with lots of white teeth – a perfect character out of an optimistic canvas from the socialist realist era.

"Are those your puppies?" he asked, pointing to the suddenly alert Belyak, who was leaping about.

Not far away, Grenlan was timidly wagging her tail.

"Yes, they're ours," I replied with a smile.

He took fifty rubles out of his pocket:

"Will you sell me the boy? Is it a boy?"

"Yes, it's a boy. I'll give him to you for free."

"No-no, it's yours... I'll take him to the country. Some jerks in the village shot all the dogs."

"I don't want it."

I scooped up Belyak and put him on the man's lap, and at this moment the man managed to shove a fifty-ruble coin into the hand that was holding Belyak under his stomach, and pressed my palm so hard with his rough hand, as if he wanted to say: "I'm having a good day, buddy, take the money, I tell you." After this gesture, it was awkward to give it back. So I took it.

"Marysenka, we have money to buy ice-cream," I said, running into the house.

"Valies is dead," said Marysenka.

"So, princess, you're left all alone?" I patted Grenlan.

She had finally got used to people patting her. Although she looked at me with alarm, she didn't roll on her back or piddle anymore. Her whole expression was full of uncommon gratitude. I didn't know what to do with myself. I went to Marysenka. She was lying down, because she felt sorry for Valies.

I went up the staircase slowly, like an old man. I said quietly: "Today's... a nasty.. day..." There was a step for each word. "Grasshoppers'... choir... sleeps": another three steps. And the same lines for the next six steps. I didn't remember the rest, and for a change I tried to read the poem backwards: "sleeps… choir… grasshoppers", but discovered that you could only read it like that if you were going downstairs.

I slowed down in front of the door: I couldn't work out how I should react to Valies' death. I'd only seen him once in my life. It was easiest not to react at all. I slowed down some more, taking the keys out of my pocket and examining each key on the key-ring, touching the jagged edge with the tip of the index finger of my left hand.

In the entranceway the door suddenly slammed, and someone downstairs shouted hoarsely;

"Hey! Someone's killing your dog!"

I tore downstairs. The lines that I had just been repeating scattered in different directions. I ran outside and in front of me stood a man who looked like an alcoholic – he seemed familiar to me.

"Where?" I shouted at him.

"There's a woman there…" He was breathing heavily. "Over there…" – he pointed. "A boxer…"

I could already hear a dog's squeal, and tearing toward this squeal through the bushes, I immediately saw everything. My Grenlan was being mauled by a boxer – a stocky, broad-chested, tailless beast. With a collar. The boxer evidently had first siezed her silly, pathetic snout and torn the poor dog's lip. Her torn lip was bleeding. A savage yelp issued forth from our little dog's open mouth, and stayed on the same note for an unnaturally long time, momentarily falling silent and then renewing again on an even higher note.

I don't know how she tore her snout out of the boxer's mouth, but now, constantly yelping, Grenlan was trying to crawl away on her front paws. The boxer had sunk his teeth into her back leg. Her leg was unnaturally twisted to the side, as if it had already been bitten through. "If I hit the boxer in the snout now, he'll bite the leg off!" I thought miserably.

I looked from side to side, trying to find a stick, something that I could use to unclench his jaws, and noticed a fat, well-dressed woman standing some distance away. She had a leash in her hand, and was playing with it. *Hey, that's her dog!*

"What are you doing, bitch?" I screamed, and distinctly realized that I was going to kill both the woman and her dog.

The woman smiled, looking at the dogs, and even whispered something. She was distracted by my shout.

"What do you want?" she said disdainfully. "Breeding all kinds of carrion here."

"You're carrion yourself, bitch!" I shouted, grabbed a hefty piece of white brick off the ground, and stepped towards the woman, who maintained a calm and disdainful expression on her face, but then I remembered my little dog who was being attacked.

Without letting go the piece of brick, I leaped over to the dogs, and with all my strength, without even thinking about what I was doing, I whacked the boxer in the snout. With a yelp, the boxer opened his jaws, and jumping back, he stood to the side. It seemed to me that he was licking his lips.

"Don't touch him! I'll set him on you, scum!" I heard the woman's voice.

Ignoring her shout, I threw the brick and hit the dog in the side.

"Yes!" I gave a hoarse, happy shout.

The dog yelped – it spat blood and ran into the bushes.

I hope I've ruptured his liver…

I didn't see where Grenlan went, all I remember is that as soon as the boxer released her, she limped off somewhere on three paws, hurrying away in deathly terror, looking back and rolling her enormous eyes. Although her fourth leg did not fall off, it was twisted so terribly that it did not even touch the ground.

The woman shouted at me with a well-modulated voice. I didn't understand what she was shouting, I didn't care. I found the piece of brick I'd thrown and turned to her, raising the trembling hand that was holding the shard.

"I'm going to knock your block off," I said clearly and quietly. My heart was thumping.

"You'll put you in jail, you bastard!" she screamed, looking at me wildly, but still disdainfully.

"And they'll lay you!... Take that!" I shouted at her and threw the stone at her feet. It bounced and hit her under the knee.

Blood from the wound immediately flowed down her torn stocking. The blow made her take two steps back and she stood motionless, looking through me, as if looking at me was beneath her dignity. I jumped over and picked up the brick again, although I could have hit her with my fist, but I didn't want to. I wanted to pound her with the brick. But my initial malice had ebbed, and I realized, I sensed that no – I couldn't do it anymore.

"Fuck you!" I shouted again, raising my hand with the brick in it. "Fuck you!"

She turned around and walked away. She wanted to carry her head straight, lift it up high and disdainfully – probably the way that she had held it for a long time, but fear made her sink her head into her shoulders – and so, torn between her arrogance and her fear, she twitched like a goose. I spat after her, but didn't reach her, the wind blew my spit away.

Grenlan... Where's our girl? I remembered, and ran into our yard, but didn't find anyone there. *Where is she?*

I squatted on the grass in the yard. I felt like smoking. I squatted, twitching nervously and listening to my heart, which was pounding in my temples. I caught my breath and went to look for the dog. I walked around the neighborhood until dark. I came home empty-handed.

Marysenka slept uneasily during the night, and when I placed my hand on her chest, I felt her heart beating.

"Shall we go to Valies?" she said in the morning.

We put on dark clothing and went.

... The coffin had been carried out of the house, it stood by the entranceway. We squeezed through to the deceased through several dozen people surrounding the coffin. As we squeezed through,

I heard the words *heart..., heart attack* and *he could have lived longer...* No one was crying. Valies' face was stern. His neck, which had been so large during his life, and which seemed to preserve an unusual wealth of modulations, was sunken in. There was nowhere for his voice to fit anymore. People whispered and shuffled. I wanted it to start raining. We left the crowd.

"Shall we go to the cemetery?" I asked Marysenka.

She shook her head no. We walked farther away from the people and stood by the swings. I rocked one of them. There was an unpleasant squeak, that sounded especially harsh in the silence that prevailed all around. My heart skipped a beat. The swings continued to rock, but without any sound.

We headed home. We turned the corner of the building, hugged and kissed.

"I love you," I said.

"I love you," she said

"What day of the week is today?" I asked

Marysya looked at the dark gray street. There was almost no one around.

"Today is Monday," she said. Although it was Saturday.

"And tomorrow?" I asked.

Marysenka was silent for a moment – not thinking about what day it would be tomorrow, but rather deciding whether or not to reveal the truth to me.

"There won't be any Sunday," she said.

"What will there be?"

Marysenka looked at me thoughtfully and tenderly, and said:

"There will be more happiness. More and more of it."

Sin

He was seventeen, and he carried his body nervously.

His body consisted of an Adam's apple, sturdy bones, long arms, absentminded eyes, and an overheated brain.

In the evenings, when he lay down to sleep in his hut, he listened to the words spinning around in his head *and he died… he… died…*

He tried to imagine how someone would cry, and how his cousin, whom he youthfully, brokenly, strangely loved, would scream. He is lying there dead, and she is screaming.

Somewhere in the hazy heat of his brain he already understood that he would never kill himself; he lived so gently and passionately, he was of a different constitution, he had warm blood, which was destined to flow easily in its course around his body, and wouldn't escape through a vein, or a slit throat, or a punctured chest.

He listened to the inner pulsing *he died… died,* and he drifted off, alive, with outstretched arms. That's how you sleep when you're condemned to happiness, to the gentleness of others, accessible and light to the taste.

Sometimes rats would run along the wooden flooring.

Grandma poisoned the rats, sprinkling something white in the corners. They ate it at night, cursing and squeaking.

In the mornings he washed himself in the yard, listening to the morning talk: the timid goat, the lively pig, the pushy rooster. And once he forgot to close the door to the hut. He stepped in to find the stupid chickens bustiling about near the poison.

He shooed them away, clucking as they went (the stern rooster in the yard answered them). Hopping, shedding feathers, and unable to find the door (the rooster crowing constantly in the yard, the feather-brained poser), the hens finally darted out into the yard.

For a long time, probably for several hours, he was worried that that the chickens would grow melancholy, just as every animal does before death, and then croak: Grandma would be upset. But the chickens survived – maybe they hadn't eaten much, or more likely, their bird brains were too tiny to understand that they had been poisoned.

The rats survived too, but they began moving much slower, as if they were perpetually lost in thought and no longer in a hurry to go anywhere.

One night, frightened by some rustling, he tuned on the light in the hut. It seemed that the rat was running, but it just couldn't cross the room. Looking at the unexpected light, it lost its way, and took a strange ring-shaped route, as if it were in the circus.

He grabbed the poker, stretched out his skinny body with its skinny muscles, and hit the rat across the back, and again, and again.

Squatting down, he looked at the sly, half-closed eye, the repugnant tail. He lifted the dead body with the poker, took it out to the yard, and stood, barefoot, looking at the stars with the dead rat.

Since then, he stopped saying at night *...he... died...*

When he woke up, he would close the squeaky door to the hut where he spent his days and nights, not bothering anyone, reading, looking at the ceiling, corner, and fooling around, and went into the house, where Grandma had gotten up a long time ago to milk the goat, let the hens out, shoo the ducks to the river, and make breakfast. Grandpa would sit at the table with his rimless spectacles on his nose, fixing something and breathing loudly.

He would glance into the large room, see Grandpa's back, and immediately disappear without a sound, afraid that he might be asked to help. He could take things apart, but putting them back together again... the details lost their meaning, even though just a few minutes ago it had seemed that the pattern was simple and clear. The only thing left then was to sweep away the metal trifles with his hand and irrevocably throw it all into another trash bin, ashamed of himself and smiling stupidly.

"You're up?" Grandma would sy affably, moving quietly, never fussing over the stove.

He would sit down at the table in the small kitchen, watching the winged trajectories of the flies. Then he would get up and grab a swatter – a wooden stick with a black rubber triangle on top, which crushed the flies into pulp with a loud whack.

Killing the flies was an amusement, maybe even a game. The time when he used to play games was not far away at all, he could still reach it. Sometimes in the attic, where he would go searching for old, dusty (and thus even more desirable) books, he would find metal cars without wheels, and was tortured with the desire to take them to his hut, if not to drive them around the floor, at least to admire them.

Grandma was good at keeping silent, and her silence did not require a response.

The potatoes fried, crackling and firing salutes, when she lifted the lid and stirred them.

The salted cucumbers limply lay on the plate, swimming in their weak brine. The lard gathered warmth, softening and spreading its aroma after the coldness from which it had been removed.

He would wave the flies away from the table, and suddenly look with interest at the swatter, at the thin, sturdy, wooden stick that cut into the black triangle.

Dropping the swatter, he would wrinkle his face in disgust, wiping his hand on his shorts and sucking in his belly. There was a pain in his chest as if he had drunk a class of ice-cold water (but there was no remaining taste of moisture, just an oppressive pain).

Why am I given this... Why are we all given this... Couldn't it somehow be otherwise?

"Is Grandpa going to eat breakfast?" Grandma would ask, turning off the burner.

"Of course he is," the grandson would answer cheerfully, glad to be distracted from himself. He knew Grandpa never sat down at the table without him.

He would go into the room and loudly shout:

"Grandma says to come and eat!"

"Eat?" Grandpa would reply pensively. "I don't really want to… well, alright, let's go sit down." He would take off his glasses, carefully laying down the screwdriver and the pliers, and stand up with a grunt. His slippers slapped across the floor.

Calmly, with a light, gooselike movement, he would bow his head in the doorway and enter the kitchen. With the passing glance of a proprietor he looked the table over, as if checking to see if something was missing. But everything was always in its place, and seemed to have been there for decades.

"You wouldn't like a drink, Zakharka?" he would ask with well-concealed craftiness.

"No, not in the morning," the grandson would answer briskly.

Grandpa would give a barely perceptible nod: a good answer. He ate with dignity, with the occasional stern glance at Grandma. He asked about some household matter.

"Sit where you are!" Grandma would reply. "As if I wouldn't know what to feed the chickens if you weren't around..."

An almost undetectable expression crossed grandfather's face: *…foolish woman… always been foolish…* he seemed to be saying. But it ended there.

The old couple never argued. Zakharka loved them with all his heart.

"I think I'll go visit my cousins", he said to Grandma, after finishing his breakfast.

"Go on," Grandma quickly answered. "And bring them back for lunch."

His cousins lived right here in the village, two houses away. The younger one, Ksyusha, was short and pretty, with crafty eyes. She had just reached adulthood. The older one, with the gentle eyes, was the dark-haired Katya, five years her sister's senior.

Ksyusha would go to the dance hall on the other side of the village, and return at four in the morning. But she didn't sleep much, and always woke up discontented, examining herself for a long time in a hand mirror, sitting next to the window so the daylight would fall on her face.

By noon she would be in a good mood, and looking attentively into the eyes of her visiting cousin, flirting with him, asking personal questions and desiring to hear honest answers.

Her cousin, who has come for the summer, understood that Ksyusha had just recently experienced something important, something female, and that she was glad of it. She felt more self-confident, as if she had gained one more interesting support in life.

Her cousin ducked the questions, and was happily sidetracked by a bare-legged kid, Katya's three-year-old son Rodik.

The older sister's husband was serving his second year in the army.

Rodik spoke very little, although it was high time that he did. He tenderly referred to himself as

"Odik," with a tiny, barely audible "k" on the end. He understood everything, but did not remember his papa.

Zakharka played with him, sitting him on his shoulders, and they wandered around the neighborhood, this suntanned young man and the white child with puffy hair.

Katya sometimes came out of the house to respond to Ksyusha. Zakharka heard: *Well, of course you're the smartest one of us in the room…* or: *I don't care what else you do, but you're going to peel some potatoes!*

Her severity wasn't very serious.

She came out and watched intently as Zakharka, with Rodik on his shoulders, walked slowly towards the house.

"Stones," said Zakharka.

"Tones," Rodik repeated.

"Stones,", Zakharka repeated.

"Tones," Rodik agreed.

They were walking over gravel.

Zakharka understood that Katya was thinking about something important while watching them. But he didn't take any time to consider what that might be. He liked to take it easy, lazing in the sun, never thinking about anything too seriously.

"I suppose you merry-makers are hungry?", said Katya in a clear chesty voice, smiling.

"Grandma invited us to eat with them," answered Zakharka, without smiling.

"Oh well, fine. Miss Priss refuses to do any work in the kitchen anyway."

"My name is Ksyusha", her sister answered with all the seriousness of a 16-year-old, walking out of the house. She had already fastened on a skirt, carefree in the wind, flitted into a pair of little shoes, and had on a t-shirt that invariably exposed her belly. Her face remarkably reflected two emotions at once: vexation with her sister, and intrigue at the presence of her cousin.

See how stupid she is, Zakharka! said her entire look.

But look how cute my tummy is, and everything else... Zakharka seemed to read, but he wasn't completely sure if he understood correctly. Just in case, he turned away.

"In the meantime we'll go eat some apples, right, Rodik?" he said to the boy sitting on his shoulders.

"I'll go with you too," Katya attached herself.

"Le's go" Rodik replied belatedly, to Katya's delight. It was the first time she had heard him use the phrase.

The walked through the orchard, looking at apples which were still green and heavy, and the yellow sort, and then headed towards the apple tree which bore fruit that was already good and sweet in July.

"Apples," repeated Zakharka distinctly.

"Apoos," Rodik agreed.

Katya was overcome with youthful, bright, rich motherly laughter.

When Zakharka took a bite of a firm apple plucked from the branch, it occurred to him that Katya's laughter resembled that moist, fresh, crisp whiteness.

"Us little ones, we can't reach the branches," joked Katya, picking up the fruits that had fallen overnight. She liked them softer, redder.

They took turns feeding small pieces of apple to Rodik, who had been placed on the ground (Zakharka was afraid that the branches in the orchard might accidentally scratch the boy).

Sometimes, without noticing, they both fed him a piece of apple at the same time: the compliant Rodik stuffed his mouth with both pieces and chewed, staring raptly.

"Ooh", he said, pointing to an apple that had not yet been picked from the branch.

"You want me to pick that one too? What a little... carnivore," answered Zakharka sternly; he liked being somewhat stern and a bit morose when inside everything was bubbling from joy and the irrepressible charm of life. When else could you be a little morose, if not at seventeen? And especially at the sight of women.

A little later Ksyusha showed up in the orchard: she was bored at home by herself. Plus there was her cousin...

"Did you peel the potatoes?" asked Katya.

"I told you, I just painted my nails, I can't. What, do I have to repeat it ten times?"

"You can tell Father about your nails. He'll cut them for you."

Ksyusha picked an apple from another tree – not the one that her older sister liked. She didn't want to follow her example in any way. She ate grudgingly, all the while looking at her cousin.

"Are the green ones tasty?", asked Katya with charming spite, sqinting her eyes to look at Ksyusha.

"Are yours full of worms?" asked the younger sister.

At lunch time they went to the old people. The sisters immediately made peace when the discussion turned to village gossip.

"Alka's with Seryoga," Katya claimed.

"No way. He and Galka were going to get married. The matchmakers already made their rounds," Katya said in disbelief.

"I'm telling you! They rode by on a motorcycle yesterday."

"Maybe he was just taking her somewhere."

"At three in the morning," Ksyusha replied mockingly. "Across the bridges..."

Across the bridges meant the cozy fields where young villagers in love drove on motorcycles or walked to in pairs.

Zakharka looked at the sisters and thought that both Katya and Ksyusha had been "across the bridges." He imagined for one painful moment the lifted skirts, hot mouths and heavy breathing, and shook his head, driving away the distraction, such a sweet distraction that it was almost unbearable.

He held back a bit, looking at the ankles and calf muscles of the sisters. He saw the frog-like, tanned ankles of Ksyusha, and through Katya's dress full of sunlight, her hips, which only looked better since she had given birth.

He wished that the river were closer, just a few paces away. He would run and dive in and not come up to the surface for a long time, moving very slowly, touching the sandy bed, seeing elusive fishes in the cloudy semidarkness.

"Why aren't you keeping up?" asked Ksyusha, turning around.

Zakharka wished that Katya had asked this question.

Katya was talking to Rodik.

"Shall we go swimming?" he suggested, instead of answering.

"Will you carry Rodik there?" asked Katya, turning around. She took a few steps backward along the street, smiling at her cousin.

Zakharka broke into a smile, against his morose will.

"No. Pro. Blem." he answered, looking Katya in the eye.

Rodik, copying his mother, also turned around and started walking backwards, but turning around every second he immediately got tangled in his own legs and fell over. Everyone laughed.

There were too many of them to fit in the kitchen, and they ate in the big room, at a long table covered with a flowered plastic tablecloth which had been accidentally cut with a knife here and there, and also had a half-moon burned into it from the edge of a hot frying pan.

The sisters crunched on crisp cucumbers.

Zakharka liked their wonderful appetite.

It was very sunny.

Katya put some potatoes on a small plate for Rodik. He began poking and pushing them around with his fingers, all covered in lard and butter, and constantly spilled potatoes in his lap. Katya gathered the potato off her child's leg and ate it, beaming.

Zakharka sat across from them, gazing at them, and silently rubbed the sole of his foot against Katya's leg. She didn't move her leg, seemingly paying no attention to her cousin at all. She kept goading her little sister, listened to her grandmother relate something about the neighbor, and didn't neglect to admire Rodik. But she didn't look at Zakharka at all.

But he didn't take his eyes off her.

Ksyusha noticed, jealously.

The bread tasted very good. The potatoes were amazingly sweet.

They ate from a common frying pan, huge, reliable, and scarred with burn marks.

"Tomorrow Grandpa's going to kill the pig," said Grandma.

"Oh, I'm glad you reminded me," said Katya.

"Why?" asked Grandma.

"I won't come over tomorrow. I can't watch that."

"Who's forcing you, don't go out into the yard and don't watch," Grandma laughed.

"I'm not coming over either," said Ksyusha, agreeing for the first time with her sister.

The sisters helped clear the table. While they were doing so, Zakharka was outside making a bow, more for himself than for Rodik. What good would a bow be to Rodik anyway. How could he handle one?

The boy, however, steadily watched as Zakharka worked: as he found and cut down a suitable bough, and bending it wound some twine around it, held in place by notches he had cut beforehand.

"Bow", said Zakharka clearly. "Bo-ow!"

"Ow," repeated Rodik.

"You'll get him talking soon", said Katya, who had come out.

"Going hunting?" asked Ksyusha, who soon followed her sister. "Can I go? Rodik, will you take me?"

Rodik looked at Ksyusha without blinking. Zakharka looked at Katya without blinking.

"In any case you still have to peel the potatoes," said Katya, "before we go swimming. Or Papa will have nothing to eat..."

They dropped by the sisters' house. Katya set a bucket of water, the bucket with the potatoes, and a pot on the floor. Everyone sat down, and Katya handed out knives. To Ksyusha she gave the smallest, irreparably blunt. Ksyusha, cursing, went to get a different knife.

The three of them peeled the potatoes, laughing about something or other. Rodik ran among them. Katya fed him pieces of raw potato.

Ksyusha admonished her:

"What are you doing? Some mother you are! How did they trust you with a child..."

"Just make sure they don't trust you with one," answered Katya, blowing a fallen strand of hair from her face and then pushing it back in place with the wrist of the hand holding the knife.

Zakharka was enjoying himself and tried not to look at the sisters' knees: Ksyusha's were tanned, while Katya's were whiter. Katya's were round, while Ksyusha's bones jutted out daintily, like some tall-legged creature, perhaps a deer...

Also, Katya was sitting a bit farther away from the bucket of potatoes, and when she bent over…

My God, why are you pestering me with this…

Zakharka went outside. The chickens were slowly wandering about, stupid from the heat.

"Akhaka!" laughed Katya from inside the house, her voice coming nearer. "Did you hear what he said? 'Ere Akhaka?' Here's your Akhaka, Rodik! Here he is."

Rodik ran out on his staggering legs, with his sunny eyelashes and ears covered in fluffy hair.

It was ten minutes' walk to the river. Zakharka took off his shorts and with a running jump threw himself in the water, so as not to see the sisters getting undressed. *I wish I didn't have to see them at all…* he thought joyfully, and immediately turned towards the sound of their voices.

"How's the water?" the sisters asked at the same time, looked at each other angrily at first, as if suspecting mockery, but then laughed.

They didn't argue any more that day.

Katya had brought some apples with her. Lying on the bank, wriggling their feet in the sand, they ate the rosy fruit. Zakharka threw the core into the water.

"Why'd you do that?" said Ksyusha, with mild disgust.

"The fish will eat it."

Katya sat up every minute or so and yelled:

"Rodik, don't go in too deep! There are fish there! Hey!"

"There?" asked Rodik, pointing to the middle of the river, and inspired, walking in further.

"Zakharka, tell him, he'll only listen to you."

Gnawing on an apple core, her cousin was looking at how a few black curls had fought their way out of Katya's bathing suit, clinging to her white, damp leg covered in shimmering golden drops.

"Rodik!" he yelled, loud enough even to surprise himself, and the boy jumped.

"Lord, why are you yelling like that?" said a startled Katya, quickly rising from the sand.

"I'll go, you lie back down…" Zakharka went out to Rodik. "Shall we pick some cattails?" he suggested. "We already have a bow. Now we need some arrows."

"Le's go", answered Rodik readily, and climbed out of the water.

The walked along the bank, the small, innocent little paw in the youthful hand with its strange line of fate and deep life line.

They returned with cattail stalks broken for arrows. Along the way, Zakharka found a cord and wound it around one of the stalks.

"Well, froggies, have you found your bridegroom?" he asked, pulling on the bow string.

The sisters turned around, smiling languidly. He raised the bow in the air and shot a cattail stalk, which flew unexpectedly high.

Rodik immediately lost sight of the arrow, and not understanding where it could have gone, looked around in surprise.

He was awoken by the squealing of the pig.

"They're slaughtering it already! Damn, I missed it."

He jumped up from the bed and pulled on his shorts, almost falling over.

But the pig had only been tied up: with tightly pulled ropes cutting into its fatty hide, it stood in the darkness of the barn and started squealing every time it saw a human.

Zakharka watched it, standing in the doorway with his eyes only slightly pried open, without having yet washed his face, smiling.

There was not a single thought in his head, but somewhere underneath his heart he felt quietly pusling into his blood the strange sweet taste of the death of another, even an animal.

Screaming, pig? You want to live? Something was quivering in the dark and secret convolution of his brain.

Although reason, clear human reason, told him: you should feel pity, how can you not feel pity?

It's a shame, he agreed easily..

And in fact it was hard to stand the squealing for long.

He slammed the door shut and approached his grandfather, who was sitting on a stump. Grandpa was sharpening an already sinister knife, constantly reflecting sunlight off its long blade.

Grandpa sternly refused to look at Zakharka.

"How does it know it's going to be slaughtered?" asked Zakharka loudly, as soon as the squealing died down.

For a second, Grandpa raised his small and, Zakharka thought, for some reason unfriendly eyes. He stood up, and wandered over to his workshop.

He didn't hear me, thought Zakharka.

"An animal knows everything," said Grandpa softly, almost to himself, not addressing anyone.

In a minute he returned, and Zakharka understood that he had been wrong to think Grandpa was in a bad mood.

"You've never seen a pig being slaughtered?" Grandpa asked simply.

"No," Zakharka replied happily.

Grandpa nodded. It was unclear what that meant: *well, today you will,* or *good thing you haven't.*

Grandma appeared, clanging metal basins, of which she had managed to bring six at once.

She looked at Grandpa slowly puttering about, but she didn't hurry him, although she had no desire to listen to the incessant squealing.

Zakharka hovered for a minute and decided to go to the outhouse.

The welcoming wooden hut covered on the inside with old wallpaper stood near the garden. On his way there, Zakharka always looked at the rows of watermelons.

The watermelons were insultingly small and green.

They won't ripen before I leave. They won't, Zakharka thought as usual, dejected.

It was dark inside the outhouse, but the sunlight came in through the spaces between the boards. There were always one or two heavy flies flying about. They never sat still for more than a few seconds. Again they would start their furious buzzing.

There was an old *"Rural Mechanics Journal"* hanging on a nail. Zakharka looked through it for the umpteenth time, understanding nothing. In this incomprehension, the lazy skimming of dusty pages, the sunny cracks, the wayward flies, the closeness of the wooden walls, the yellowed wallpaper peeling here and there, the rusty bolt, the ceiling covered in tarred black roofing paper so it wouldn't leak – in everything there was a quiet, almost unattainable lyrical beneficence.

The pig's cries were becoming eerier, more frightening, more detached. Zakharka hurried.

The squealing was cut off before he got there. He had to let Grandma pass too: she was hurrying somewhere, and by the look of her – a bit agitated but calmer at the same time (*...it's all over, thank God...*) – Zakharka understood that the pig had been slaughtered.

With his red hands, Grandpa slowly untied (he could have cut them, but didn't, in order to preserve the rope) the knots that were holding the pig to the drainpipe of the barn.

Did he intentionally not wait for me?... or was it unintentional? thought Zakharka, and could not figure out the answer.

First the pig's backside started sagging as it was freed, but the pig was still held up, still tied by its huge neck to the pipe. Grandpa moved the basin, full of the blood that had poured from the slit throat, and undid the knot around the neck. The pig fell with a soft sound.

Zakharka went closer, looking with interest at the now-silent animal. An ordinary pig, just dead. With an even slit across the throat and a lot of white fat.

"I can't seem to find the knife," Grandpa, looked around. "Zakharka, look for it."

The knife had been stuck into the barn wall. Its handle was warm, and the blade was covered in drying blood.

He gave Grandpa the knife, holding it by the sharp end. He got his fingers smeared, and later he looked at them.

They sliced open the pig's stomach. It lay there, fallen open, exposed, red, raw. The insides were warm; you could warm your hands in them. If you squinted at them through a lightheaded haze, they might look like a bouquet of flowers. A warm bouquet of living, fleshy, bestial flowers.

Grandpa confidently removed the heart, kidneys, and liver, and threw them in basins. The contents of the large intestine he squeezed out by hand.

The living being that sullenly greeted Zakharka in the mornings, that rubbed its sides on the barn wall, that excitedly snorted upon seeing a bucket with slop, that was capable, in the end, of screaming with such unexpected power – that being turned out to be insignificant, worthless. You could slice it open, dismember it, and take out parts of it.

And here it was already, lying there cut off, the stupid pig head, with its snout up in the air, mouth open. It seemed as if the pig wanted to scream, that it was just about to let out a squeal.

And seeing that head, even the chickens were a bit stupefied, and the rooster avoided walking near, and the goat looked out from the dark with suffering Judaic eyes.

Zakharka went inside. Grandmother, hurrying to meet him with a rag in her hand, said:

"Eat, I left some food in there…"

But he didn't. And not because he had lost his appetite at the sight of the slaughtered pig. He couldn't wait to go to his cousins. Everything that was alive, that was glutted with life in its most real, primitive form, and was completely deprived of a soul – everything with those bright, colored, fragrant insides, with legs spread wide apart, with a senselessly turned up head, and with the clean smell of fresh blood, hindered him from staying in the same place, pulled him, diverted him, seethed inside him.

That same onerous pain, as if from ice water, that had been torturing him, was unexpectedly replaced with a feeling of delightful anticipatory heat. The heat was in his hands, his heart, his kidneys, his lungs: Zakharka saw his organs clearly, and they looked exactly the same as those that were steaming in front of him a minute ago. And from this realization of his own warm animal nature Zakharka felt his heart contracting, with particular passion and without pain, his real, fleshy heart, pumping blood to his arms, to his hot palms, and to his head, scalding his brain, and below, to his belly, where everything was… proud with the realization of eternal youth.

For some reason he grabbed the bow that was lying near the house, and started off with a feeling as if he had just killed an animal. And he didn't find himself ridiculous at all.

He saw Rodik first, scaring off the chickens which were already afraid of him anyway. He was hardly able to keep himself from telling Rodik what it had been like. He even let a few syllables slip, and then cut himself off, idly moving his awkward lips.

Ksyusha came out. Katya followed her.

"Well, have they killed the pig?" asked Katya, widening her eyes, and with a look as if the dead pig was going to show up right there, snorting and squelching about with its slit throat.

Ksyusha also looked frightened:

"We could hear the squealing from here. Katya and I closed all the doors and windows," she said.

Zakharka looked at the sisters, his happy eyes moving from one pretty face to the other – it was wonderful, and he looked for the word that he should start with to explain about his heart, his throat, his blood… but then in a second, he suddenly understood that he had nothing to say.

"Do you have any empty cans?" he asked.

"Yes," answered Ksyusha, shrugging her shoulders. "I think there were some over there in the trash."

Zakharka cut the lids off of three cans. He cut each of the lids in half with big scissors. With some flat-nosed pliers he curled them around yesterday's cattails and hammered the resulting spike.

The sisters went off to attend to their affairs, and only Rodik was left pattering around, repeating sometimes "Ow!" and responding to Zakharka's "Arrows! Say: arrows!" with a long, doubtful silence.

"Ah-ah."

"Exactly", agreed Zakharka.

He stretched the bow string, and released the arrow. It soared swiftly, then it seemed to pause for a moment in the air, and gently fell down, sticking into the ground.

"Wow," said Ksyusha, coming out on to the porch with a mop. "That's beautiful."

Swaying in the breeze, the arrow stuck up into the air.

"It's standing up," Ksyusha added dreamily.

She's in a good mood today, Zakharka thought. *She's washing the floors.*

He couldn't resist, and asked:

"Why are you doing the dirty work?"

"We're starting renovations today. Our Ksyusha is so eager to paint her room orange that she's prepared to make any sacrifice," Katya replied for Ksyusha.

Ksyusha, offended by her sister and cousin, squeezed the dirty water out of the mop.

Zakharka wandered around the garden, reluctantly munching on an apple.

He carried Rodik around on his shoulders, and then the boy was sent off to nap. Zakharka, in order not to get in the way of the energetically tidying sisters, went back to his room.

In the yard, Grandma had already wiped away the blood, and nothing was left of the pig: only meat in basins.

He entered the hut, creaking open the door.

It was stuffy inside. He pulled off his shorts, and climbed, somewhat disheveled, out of his t-shirt. He fell on the bed, bouncing on its springs. He turned over on his side, and reached out for an old book with a tattered cover and missing many pages, but did not take it up. He rested his cheek against the pillow, and lay still. He suddenly remembered that he hadn't had enough sleep, and closed his eyes, immediately seeing Katya, nothing but Katya…

He lay there, remembering the sound of squealing in the morning, the flight of the arrow, the black water from the mop, the taste of the apple, the apple tree is shaking and swaying, the bark is near, the dark bark, the rough bark, the bark, the bark…

The door squeaked, and he woke up instantly. *Katya,* his heart skipped a beat.

Ksyusha came in, wearing a funny bathing suit: all string ties and bows.

Prying open his eyes, Zakharka looked at her.

"Did I wake you up, were you asleep?" she asked quickly.

He didn't answer, and stretched.

"We were going swimming," Ksyusha added, sitting on the bed so that her hip touched her cousin's hip. "The paint is giving us a headache: we started painting. The doors."

Zakharka nodded and stretched again.

"Why don't you say anything?" Ksyusha asked. "Why are you always silent?" she repeated more cheerfully, and at a higher pitch – in the voice that usually precedes action. And it did: Ksyusha lightly threw her left leg over Zakharka and sat on his legs, firmly resting her hands on his knees, pressing them lightly. She looked as if she was getting ready to jump.

I didn't think I was silent... Zakharka thought, looking his cousin over with interest.

From time to time he felt her cold, firm buttocks with the soles of his feet, she rocked gently from side to side on her bottom, and suddenly sat higher, unacceptably higher – she pressed her legs against his hips and gently tickled Zakharka under his armpits.

"Are you ticklish?" she asked, and without a pause: "You've got such a hairy chest... Like a sailor. Where are you going to serve in the army? Will you join the sailors? They'll take you."

Ksyusha looked completely calm, as if nothing unusual was happening.

But while she moved and wriggled on top of him, Zakharka clearly felt that under the fabric of her funny outfit, all in bows, there was something alive, very alive...

This continued just until both of them realized that it couldn't go on like this anymore, that they needed to do something else, something impossible.

Ksyusha looked down at him with calm and clear eyes.

"I don't feel comfortable like this," Zakharka suddenly said. He made Ksyusha get off and sat opposite her, pressing his knees to his chest.

They talked for another two minutes, and Ksyusha left.

"Well, shall we go swimming?" she asked when she was outside, turning around.

"Sure, let's go," Zakharka replied, accompanying her to the door.

"Then I'll call Katya. And we'll come by to get you." With a wag of her bows, Ksyusha went out of the yard.

"I'll call Katya…" he repeated meaninglessly, like an echo.

He went to the wash basin, which resembled an upside-down German helmet. An iron rod stuck out of a hole in the center of the basin. If you raised it, water flowed out.

Zakharka stood motionless, closely looking over the wash basin, running the end of his tongue over the back of his teeth. He raised the iron rod it little: it gave a weak jangle. There was no water. He pulled the rod down.

Unexpectedly, he noticed a dried bloodstain on it.

"Grandpa probably tried to wash his hands when he slaughtered the pig…" he guessed.

In the evening Ksyusha went out dancing, and Katya and Rodik came to stay the night with Grandma and Grandpa, so the little boy wouldn't get ill from the strong smells of the renovations.

The meal lasted a long time. Lethargic from the food, they talked tenderly. The votive light by the icon flickered. Zakharka, having drunk three half shot glasses with Grandpa, looked at the icon for a long time, sometimes seeing Katya's features in the female face, only to lose them again. Rodik did not resemble the baby at all.

He had already been sent to bed several times, but he screamed loudly in protest.

Zakharka didn't want to go to his hut, delighting in his relatives, who were somehow especially wonderful on this evening.

He suddenly had a warm and cheerful premonition of himself as an adult, perhaps even an unshaven man, with a definite smell of of tobacco, although Zakharka himself didn't smoke yet.

And there he is, unshaven, with tobacco crumbs on his lips, and Katya is his wife. And they are sitting together, and Zakharka gazes at her lovingly.

He has just arrived on a big boat, which he has rowed with one oar, bringing fish, let's say, and has taken off his tall black boots in the entry. She had wanted to help him, but he said sternly: *I'll manage myself...*

Zakharka suddenly laughed at his stupid thoughts, and Katya, who was talking animatedly with Grandma, gave him a brief look, a look that was calm and understanding, as if she knew what he was thinking, and even seemed to nod slightly: *...Well, do it yourself then... Just don't leave them in the corner like last time: they won't dry out...*

Zakharka loudly ate a pickle, to return to his senses.

Grandpa, who had got up from the table a long time ago to listen to the evening news, walked past them from the second room to go outside, talking as if to himself as usual, without malice:

"Still sitting there? As if we'd only just seen each other, just arrived..."

The conversation happened to turn to the pig that had been slaughtered earlier. Katya waved her hands to show that she didn't want to hear anything about it, and Grandma, who was unusually talkative, suddenly told a story about how a witch had lived nearby in her youth. She was ugly, bony and perpetually bareheaded, which was not the custom in the village. She dried herbs, or sometimes even mice, rats' tails, and various bones of other animals.

Among other things, people said of the old woman that she turned into a pig at night. Naughty village boys decided to find out if this rumor was true, and snuk into the old woman's yard at night, to the pig barn, and cut off the pig's ear.

Early the next morning, the old woman, who was hurrying to the river to get water at sunrise, was seen for the first time wearing a head scarf, and even under the black scarf it could be seen that her head was wrapped in a rag on one side.

Katya sat quietly, never taking her eyes off Grandma. Zakharka was looking over Katya's shoulder, out the window, and suddenly whispered:

"Katya, what's that at the window? Is it the pig looking in?"

Katya jumped up with a squeal. Grandma laughed, covering her beautiful mouth with the end of a handkerchief. Katya gasped, running from the window to the other end of the table, not completely seriously. But then she started scolding Zakharka quite sincerely:

"You idiot! I'm scared of all that stuff..."

They laughed a little more.

"Now you'll go to your hut, and the pig will bite you," Katya said quietly.

For some reason, Zakharka thought that the pig would bite him in a specific place, and that this was what Katya was talking about. Again, his heart skipped a beat, but he did not find anything to reply about the pig, because he was thinking about something quite different.

"You can sleep here," Grandma said to Zakharka, half-joking, half-serious, as if really worried that an evil spirit would bite her grandson; Grandma herself had never been scared of anything. "There's enough space, we'll make beds for everyone," she added.

"It's a big hut – there's enough room to go riding in it," Grandpa said, coming back from outside. Usually, he was half-deaf, but sometimes he unexpectedly heard things that were said quietly, and not even addressed to him.

Everyone laughed again, and even Rodik crooked his pink lips.

Grandpa had long considered his hut to be the largest, if not in the whole village, then certainly one of the largest.

If he went to visit someone, for example to a wedding, he would come back and say:

"Our hut's bigger, mother. It was kind of crowded there."

"They have four rooms, what are you talking about?" Grandma would say. "And there were forty-three guests."

"You call those rooms..." Grandpa would mumble in a bass voice. "Dog kennels, more like it."

"We had eighteen people living here, when my father was alive," he would inform Zakharka for the hundreth time, if he happened to be near. "Six sons, all with wives, mother, father, children… There were benches along every wall, we slept on them. And now she finds it crowded here with just the two of us," he would complain about Grandma.

This time he didn't mention the eighteen people, but walked past, pretending not to hear or see the laughter. He turned up the television in the other room – so that the hubbub could probably be heard in the house next door, where the alcoholic Gavrila lived, who did not have any electrical appliances.

Katya helped Grandma clear the table. Zakharka depicted a battle with forks for Rodik until the forks were also taken away from him, and put with the rest of the dirty dishes.

They went into the room, to the pillows and sheets, which always had a barely detectable, but pleasant, sour scent of mustiness: from the large chests and the pile of fabric that had lain in stuffy, close quarters for a long time.

Zakharka got the couch. He waited until the light was turned out, quickly got undressed and lay down, wrapping himself in the blanket, although it was quite warm.

Grandpa lay on his bed, and Grandma on hers. Katya and Rodik got the low bed that stood in the corner of the room, opposite Zakharka.

Zakharka lay there and listened to Katya, her breathing, her movements, her voice, when she tried to talk some sense into Rodik in a stern whisper.

As if afraid that she would see his gaze in the darkness, Zakharka did not look in Katya's direction.

Rodik refused to calm down, he was unaccustomed to being in a new place. He sat up, banged his feet on the floor, and tried to make his mother laugh, squirming on the bed. When he crawled under the blanket yet again, getting caught up in the blanket cover, Katya suddenly sat up, and there was a crack and a crash: something had broken in the wooden bed.

Rodik got a slap on his head, set up a whine, and went running to Grandma's bed.

They turned on the night lamp: the bed had collapsed on its side and could no longer be slept on.

"Go sleep with your cousin," Grandma said simply.

Zakharka moved to the edge of the sofa, his arms alongside his body, eyes on the ceilin;, but he still noticed the flash of a white triangular piece of fabric. Katya lay by the wall.

They both lay there without breathing. Zakharka knew that Katya was not asleep. He didn't feel her warmth, he didn't touch his cousin with a single millimeter of his body, but something inexplicable that emanated from her he could sense keenly, physically, with all his being.

They didn't move, and Zakharka could hear the blinking of Katya's eyelashes. Then in the darkness came the almost inaudible sound of slightly dry lips opening, and Zakharka realized that she was breathing through her mouth. He repeated this movement, and felt the air moving against his teeth, and he knew that she was feeling the same thing: the same air, the same inhalation…

Rodik lay still for about ten minutes, and it seemed that he had fallen asleep. But suddenly his voice was heard clearly:

"Mama."

"Sleep," said Grandma.

"Mama," he said insistently.

"Do you want your mama?"

"Yes. Mama," Rodik repeated clearly.

Katya didn't respond. But Rodik had already clambered over his Grandma, and guessing his way in the darkness, he reached the couch.

Zakharka picked him up and put him between himself and Katya. The boy laughed happily and with his raised legs began playing a lively game with the blanket. Especially as he felt cramped on the sofa, and his sharp elbows pressed into both his mama's and Zakharka's sides.

"No, we won't get any sleep like this," Zakharka said.

Quickly, before anyone could say anything, he went out, picking his shorts up off the floor, and saying amiably as he left:

"I'll go and pay the pig a visit. You sleep."

In the corridor, he stepped into his flip-flops, put his shorts on, cursing, and walked out the door. Outside, the night was starry, cool and joyful.

"The pig won't bite," he repeated, smiling to himself, not thinking about any pig. "It won't bite, it won't betray you, it won't eat you."

In his hut, he sat down on the bed, and swung his legs, looking as if he had found an activity to keep him occupied all night. He looked out the small window, where there was the moon and a cloud.

In the early fresh morning, Zakharka was happily painting the doors and window frames in his cousins' house.

It was slowly getting warm.

When Katya appeared in a white shirt, with the ends tied up around her waist, and in an old pair of leggings turned up at the knees, which suited her very well, he realized that he wouldn't have slept for a second if he had stayed next to her.

He laughed a lot, teasing his cousins about little things, and felt that he had become more confident and stronger, though when this had happened remained inexplicable.

Ksyusha made a few feeble brush strokes and went away somewhere.

Katya talked merrily about her sister: what she was like as a child, and how this childhood ended one summer. And she talked about herself, about the strange things she did when she was young. And even when she wasn't young.

"Idiot," Zakharka said in response to something trivial.

"What did you say?" she asked in surprise.

"You're an idiot, I said."

Katya fell silent, and went away to mix the paint. She concentrated as she stirred a stick in the can, lifting it up and watching the thick paint slowly dripping off it.

About three hours later, they were sitting on the steps of the house. Katya was peeling potatoes, and Zakharka was chewing pumpkin seeds, feeding some of them to the chickens.

"You're the first man to call me an idiot," Katya informed him seriously.

Zakharka didn't reply. He looked at her quickly and kept chewing the seeds.

"What do you think about that?" Katya asked.

"I only called you that because of something you did," he replied.

"And the worst thing is that I wasn't offended at you."

Zakharka shrugged.

"No, say something at least," Katya insisted. "...about that..."

"Would you have been offended at your beloved husband?" Zakharka asked, just for the sake of asking something.

"I love you more than I love my husband," Katya replied simply, and cut the last piece of skin off the potato.

With a gentle splash, the potato, naked like a baby, fell into the bucket.

Zakharka looked at how many seeds were left in his hand.

"What else are we going to do today?" he asked, after a silence.

Katya looked somewhere past him through clear, thoughtful eyes.

In the house, Rodik woke up and lifted his voice.

They rushed to him, almost competing, each one with their own tenderness, which was so abundant that Rodik shrank away in surprise: what's up with you?

"Shall we go for a walk?" Katya suggested. "I'm sick of working".

Along a faint path, which Zakharka had never walked on, they quietly wandered around the back of the village, with Rodik on Zakharka's shoulders, as always.

They walked through shady bushes, sometimes along a creek, and then along a quiet dusty road uphill slightly, towards the sun.

Unexpectedly for Zakharka, they reached an iron fence, and iron gates with a cross on them.

"The old cemetery," Katya said quietly.

Rodik didn't care where they were, and he ran between the graves and rusty fences, chattering in his own language.

Katya and Zakharka walked together, reading the old Russian names, calculating the years of life, delighting in the long lifespans and wondering at the short ones. They found entire families buried in the same patch of ground, old people, those who died on the day they were born, brave soldiers and young girls. They tried to guess how, and for what reason, and where it had happened.

At a grave without photos or dates, they stood pointlessly, and looked at it. Katya was in front, Zakharka was behind her, close to her, feeling the warmth of her hair and with all his hot body feeling how warm she would be, how flexible and intolerable if he embraced her... right now...

Katya stood there motionless, without saying anything, although they had just been joking incessantly.

Suddenly, Rodik came running out at them, as if from out of a hiding place, and they all livened up – initially quite randomly, pronouncing strange words, as if they were testing their throats. But then everything became better, much better, quite good indeed.

They returned feeling quite revived, as if they had just been in a very fine and welcoming place.

They took up the brushes with pleasure once more.

All that day, with its smells of paint, the unnaturally bright colors, the quick lunch – spring onions, radishes and the first young tomatoes – and then sheets of wallpaper, intoxicating glue, Rodik getting underfoot, already smeared with everything possible – in the end he was taken to Grandma – and a still ill-tempered Ksyusha ("... she had an argument with her boyfriend..." Katya whispered), and their hands, washed with gasoline in the pale summer twilight – all of this, when Zakharka finally went to bed at night, for some reason transformed into a very bright carousel, a whirligig, on which he was spinning, and wide-eyed faces flashed past, looking fixedly, but then the chairs on the long chains were taken a long way away, and only the colors remained: green, blue, green.

And only by morning, with the distant singing of birds, came an unexpected stillness, – transparent and gentle, like at the cemetery.

...Every one of my sins... Zakharka thought sleepily, *every one of my sins will torment me... And*

the good that I have done –it's lighter than fluff. It will be blown away by any draft of wind…

The following summer days, which had begun so long and slow, suddenly started to slip by unnoticeably, like the almost even circle of a whirligig, identically happy to such extent that their pattern faded.

On the last morning, alreadypacked, wearing jeans, a robust shirt, and shoes that surprised his feet, Zakharka wandered around the yard.

He wondered what else to do. He couldn't think of anything.

He found the bow and the last arrow for it. He stretched the bow string and let it go. The arrow fell in the dust, a pink feather on its end.

Like a fool, he said to himself happily. *You're behaving like a fool.*

He kissed Grandma, hugged Grandpa, and walked away, so as not to see their tears. Strong and weightless, he almost flew to the highway – the name given to the asphalt road outside the village, where a bus drove past at six in the morning.

He didn't go to say goodbye to the sisters, what was the point of waking them up.

How the starlings are screeching, he noticed on the way.

And he also thought: *The burdock is aromatic.*

He rode in the bus with a clear heart.

How right everything is, my God, he repeated serenely. *How right, my God. What a long life lies ahead. There'll be another summer, and it will be warm again, and flowers in our arms…*

But there was never another summer.

Karlsson

That spring I quit my job working as a bouncer at a bar. I was so filled with tenderness towards the world that I decided to join the foreign legion as a mercenary. I had to find some way to apply myself, by any means.

I had turned twenty-three: a strange age, when it's so easy to die. I was unmarried, physically strong, energetic and cheerful. I was good at shooting and could allow the possibility of shooting at anything, especially in another country, where there are other gods that don't care about me.

In the large city where I came from a distant suburb, there was something similar to an office of the foreign legion. They accepted my documents and talked to me about some specific issues.

I did as many push-ups as they needed, did as many chin-ups as they wanted, happily ran for five kilometers and did some other things, either jumped or did sit-ups, probably one hundred or one hundred and fifty times.

After a psychological test that was ten pages long, the psychologist raised his indifferent eyebrows at me and said tiredly: "Aren't you a person to envy… Are you really like this, or have you already taken this test?"

As I waited to be summoned to the representative office, I wandered around the city and breathed in the warmth that smelt of bushes and petrol with my young lungs, and as I gathered air into them I thought that if I wanted to, I could take off a little.

Soon after that, two weeks later, my money ran out, and I had no means of paying for the empty room I was renting, with a wonderful hard bed and two dumbbells under it, and almost nothing to feed myself with. But like any happy person, a way out of the situation found me itself, hailing me during a daily walk that was almost as long as noon.

When I heard my name, I turned around with a light heart, always prepared for everything, but at the same time not expecting anything from life but good things.

His name was Alexei.

We had once been introduced by my strange girlfriend, who embroidered pictures, I don't remember what these creations are actually called. She gave some pictures to me, and I immediately hid them in a shoebox, sincerely thinking that sewing on epaulets was much harder.

I took the box along with me. Along with the dumbbells, it was my most prized possession. Two or three semi-literate letters from comrades from my barracks past lay in the box, and a bundle of tender and heart-wrenching letters from my brother, who was in prison for committing ten, or maybe twelve, robberies.

Next to the box, there was a volume with three novels by a great Russian émigré, a soldier in the

Volunteers Army, and French taxi-driver. Reading his novels, I felt in my heart that clear and warm bitterness, almost incomprehensible to me, that spread out into a smile even as I was about to hit someone.

There was also an exercise book, in which sometimes, not more than once a week, but usually much more rarely, I sometimes wrote down rhymed lines, surprising myself. They came to me easily, but inside I realized that I didn't feel anything that I described, and had never felt it. Sometimes I reread what I had written and was surprised again: where did that come from?

I never even looked at my girlfriend's embroidered pictures.

Then she had an exhibition, and it turned out to be a lot more than epaulets, and she asked for the pictures back, but I had lost them, of course – I had to make up some lie.

But I went to the exhibition, and for some reason she introduced me to Alexei, although I didn't express any desire to be introduced to him, or to anyone at all.

At first glance, he made a strange impression. He was morbidly fat, with traces of teenage acne that had not healed. The features of his face were blurred, as though they had been drawn on wet paper.

But Alexei turned out to be a friendly sort of person, and immediately suggested that we drink at his expense somewhere nearby, and so I didn't really get a proper look at the exhibition.

For some reason, he was the person who happened to have been pushed out into to the springtime street to hail me when I had run out of money, and he loudly spoke my name.

We said hello, and he immediately squatted down to do up his shoelace. I pensively looked at the top of his head with its sparse, sweaty thin hairs – like children have, when they are almost newborn.

His head was large and round.

Then he got up, and I didn't even think of starting the conversation, but he easily started talking, he simply caught some word in the air, whatever one was closest of all, perhaps the word was *asphalt*, perhaps it was *shoelace*, and he followed it, and kept on talking. It was all the same to him what shoelace to begin with.

Without thinking it over, I agreed once more to drink at his expense.

After we drank half a bottle of vodka, and I had listened to everything that he said for about half an hour, I finally pronounced one phrase. It was simple: "Me? I live well; I just don't have a job."

He immediately offered me a job. In the same place where he worked.

We quickly became friends, I don't know what he needed me for. But he didn't depress me, didn't irritate me and even cheered me up sometimes. He liked to talk, and I didn't mind listening. Strange things were constantly happening to him – he was always falling asleep drunk in stairwells, night trains and public squares, and would wake up to find he had been robbed or beaten up, or was in the drunk tank, where he had also been robbed.

He had a gentle and quite tactful sense of humor. Sometimes his ideas about life turned into colorful aphorisms. When he was sober, he moved quickly, but only over short distances – to the smoking area, say. He smoked a lot, he liked baggy shirts, his shoes were always dusty, and always had laces.

I addressed him tenderly: Alyosha. He was just over thirty, he had graduated from the Literature Institute and had served in the army, where, in some way unfathomable to me, he had not been killed.

Our work wasn't hard. We were reinforcement workers in one of those worthless offices that have become so numerous in our strange times. They were born and died almost painlessly, although sometimes they left without pay those yawning workers who had failed to sense the approaching collapse.

In the evenings, when the workday was coming to an end, he would quietly approach me, and lean over, whispering:

"I feel sad, Zakhar. How about drinking some vodka?"

We would wander out of the office, already feeling the tender anxiety of approaching alcoholic intoxication, and that made us start talking louder, taking delight in incidental trifles.

He talked almost all of the time, I only interjected occasionally, not more than a dozen words in a row; and if what I said made him laugh, this made me happy for some reason. I didn't ask a lot from our friendship, I was used to being satisfied with what I had.

As we approaching the kiosk, Alyosha started speaking more quietly: as if he were afraid that someone would catch him buying vodka. If I didn't follow Alyosha's example of quieting down by the kiosk, and kept acting the fool, he would hush me. I would shut my mouth, staying happy on the inside. I have a strange habit of sometimes obeying good, kind, weak people.

We pitched in together to buy the vodka, usually equally – but Alyosha never trusted me to buy anything, he took the money from me and pushed me away from the window of the kiosk with a look that said unless he did everything himself, I would be sure to get confused and buy a box of candy instead.

He bought a bottle of vodka, a dark yellow bottle of lemonade and two plastic cups. Alyosha didn't believe in snacks. Afterwards – so he thought – the money left over would probably come in handy, when everything had been drunk and of course it wouldn't seem to be enough.

We would go into a quiet, neglected yard. In the corner of the yard there was an old bench – to the right of it there was a crooked old yellow building, and on the left there was a row of damp, rotting barns, where we went to urinate once we'd drunk the vodka.

As we approached the bench, he would say with relief: "Well, here we are..." In the sense that everything had worked out fine, despite my clumsy, noisy behavior, and annoying advice about buying at least something to chew on.

He always put the vodka away in his bag, and poured it out when he thought necessary.

We threw the rubbish off the bench, laid out sheets of newspapers, and joked quietly. The jokes already sounded in a different register: the throat quieted down as if it was saving itself for the burn that was soon to come, and did not effervesce so loudly and cheerfully.

We lit cigarettes, and sat for a while in silence, looking at the smoke.

Then Alyosha poured out some vodka, and I sat with my head inclined, watching the gentle flow of the clear liquid.

After the first shot, he would start coughing, and coughed for a long time, with a look of unusual disgust. I chewed on the stem of a fallen leaf, good-naturedly cursing myself for not taking a little money from Alyosha to buy myself some food.

From time to time, out of the crooked yellow building, young people would come out, hunched over, with stupid faces, wearing leggings rolled up to the knees and flip-flops; they talked loudly, tirelessly swearing and spitting on the ground.

I scowled and didn't take my eyes off them.

"Just without any excesses, Zakhar, I beg you. No excesses," Alyosha would immediately say, looking to the side, as if he did not want to catch the disgusting youths with his gaze.

"I won't do anything, I won't," I would laugh.

When I'm drunk I have a tendency to start fights, be rude and do all sorts of stupid things. But no matter what disorderly state I'm in, I would never involve this heavyset, hulking man, who probably has a diseased liver. He couldn't fight or run away – why should he have to die there because of my foolishness?

"I won't do anything," I repeated honestly.

The young guys were shouting something to their girlfriends, who appeared at various windows on the second or third floor. The girls plastered their faces against the glass; the faces displayed a strange mixture of interest and contempt. Having grimaced and given unintelligible replies, the girls went back into the depths of their nauseating apartments with an abundance of metal dishes in the kitchens. Sometimes, after the girls, the irritated faces of their mothers appeared at the window for a moment.

Finally, the guys would disperse, taking away the blisters on their knees and the nasty echo of foul, stupid swearing.

After the second shot, he cheered up, and drank with increasing ease, still with a sour squint, but no longer coughing.

As we began to feel warmer, Alyosha's terrible face turned pink, and he began to talk. The world, it seemed, had revealed itself to him anew, and was child-like and surprising. In every monologue by Alyosha, there was always a lyrical hero present – he himself, a calm, friendly, kind, non-envious person, worthy of tender love. How could you not love Alyosha, if he was so touching, soft and cheerful? So I thought.

Sometimes, out of forgetfulness, I tried to tell some story out of my own life, about my job at the bar, about the crazy things that happened there, though I had never been beaten up, and was never humiliated; but Alyosha would immediately start to fidget impatiently, and in the end he would interrupt me without hearing me out.

Having smoked again, both of us feeling extremely satisfied and tender, we would once more set off to the kiosk, looking back doubtfully at the bench: we didn't want anyone else to occupy it.

We had a tradition: we always went to a bookshop after the first bottle, but never bought anything. Alyosha only bought books when he was sober, after he had been paid, and I took them out of the library.

We simply walked around the shop, as if it were a museum. We touched the covers, opened the first pages, and looked at the author's faces.

"Do you like Hemmy?" I asked, stroking the attractive blue tomes.

"You get sick of his hero very quickly, this annoying strong guy. A beer bar, a boxing bar. Tigers and bulls. Tigers' habits, bulls' balls..."

I looked over Alyosha's figure ironically and didn't say anything. He didn't notice my irony. It seemed to me that he didn't notice it.

Alyosha himself had been writing a novel for five years now, with the fine but outdated title "*The Walrus and the Carpenter.*" I never could explain how I knew that it was outdated.

Once I asked Alyosha to read the first few chapters, and he didn't refuse. The novel featured Alyosha himself,renamed Seryozha. For several pages, Seryozha suffered from the stupidity of the world: peeling potatoes in the kitchen (I liked the "starched knives") and even sitting on the toilet – next to him, like a boil, there was a basin hanging on the wall; I also liked the boil, but not as much.

I told Alyosha about the knives and the basin. He grimaced. But after enduring a small pause of several hours, Alyosha unexpectedly inquired in a dissatisfied voice:

"You write something, don't you? And you even get published? I don't know why you need that... Maybe you'll let me read your texts?"

The next day he returned the pages to me, and mumbled, looking to the side:

"You know, I didn't like it. But don't be upset, I'll read some more."

I laughed whole-heartedly. We got into a shuttle bus, and I tried to cheer up Alyosha, as if I was guilty of something towards him.

It was a foul and sweaty summer, exhausting to itself. It smelt of gasoline inside the shuttle bus, and all the opened windows and hatches did not make it any less stuffy. We were driving over a bridge, hardly moving in an enormous, harried traffic jam. The river flowed beneath, looking as though it had had oil and gasoline poured into it.

The shuttle bus shook, overcrowded with people, who hung on to the handles with suffering faces. My Alyosha, heavy and soaked through, crushed on all sides, felt especially faint.

The driver had some loud, hoarse-voiced music playing on the tape-recorder. He was obviously keen to acquaint the entire bus with the grimly zealous gangster music he liked so much.

Stupefied by the heat, by the stuffiness, by other people's bodies, but most of all by the ghastly racket that was booming out of the driver's speakers, shutting my eyes I imagined that I was whacking the singer over the head with a heavy chair leg.

The traffic jam was steadily getting worse. Cars honked angrily and incessantly.

Alyosha stared vacantly at a spot somewhere above my head. Sweat kept pouring down his face. You could see that he was also listening to the performance, and it was making him feel ill. Alyosha chewed his lips, and said distinctly, almost syllable by syllable:

"Now I know what hell looks like to Mozart."

We couldn't bear to stay in the shuttle bus, and long before we reached the place where we worked we got out, and decided to drink some beer. My friend panted and rolled his eyes, gradually coming to life. The beer was ice-cold.

"Alyosha, you're great!" I said, admiring him.

He didn't show that he was very happy with my words.

"My fine friend, let's not go to work," Alyosha suggested. "Let's make up some lie."

We rang the office, lied to them, and didn't go to work, but sat in the shade, swigging beer.

Then we went for a walk, virtually holding each other by the arm, fully aware, but not saying it out loud, that we would be outrageously drunk by the evening.

"Look, it's our bookshop!" Alyosha said, enraptured. "Let's go and commemorate the books that we could have bought and read."

We once more wandered between the rows of books, brushing against the beautiful covers and touching the spines of the books, which, I always remember, gave out an acrid odor.

"Gaito, the magnificent Gaito… Look, Alyosha! Have you read Gaito?"

"Yes," Alyosha grimaced. "I've read him".

"And?" I raised my eyebrows, with a premonition of something.

"He's not a bad writer. But all these uninteresting, pointless descriptions of exercises on the chin-up bar... this character who is only concerned with his bravery, although it would seem that he also solves metaphysical problems... the same guy from novel to novel, who discreetly flexes his triceps and always knows how to break a person's finger... It's a secret aesthetic of violence. Remember how enthralled he is when he watches a gigolo getting beaten up?"

"Stop it, Alyosha, you're nuts," I interrupted him and left the shop, angry for no apparent reason.

My friend followed, without looking at me. He was in the mood to drink vodka and looked keenly at the kiosk, as though it might go away.

"And what about the Russian American, the butterfly enthusiast? What about his books?" I asked an hour later.

"It's strange that you know your literature," Alyosha said instead of replying. "You'd be better suited to throwing knives... or spears... And then shave your head with them. With blunt blades."

"His Russian period is especially unpleasant," Alyosha replied a minute later, pouring out the rest of the vodka. "Although I haven't read anything from his American period, apart from the novel about the little girl... But then, many Russian novels are revolting because of the narrator. A sport snob who despises all..."... - Alyosha searched for a word, and not finding it, added, "all the rest..."

"A person like you," Alyosha suddenly added in a completely sober voice, and immediately started talking about something else.

He sat on the bench, enormous and corpulent. The sides of his white, flabby body bulged out of his shirt. I smoked a lot and looked at Alyosha attentively, sometimes forgetting to listen to him.

For some reason, I remembered a story that Alyosha had told a long time ago, about his father. His father was an invalid, he did not leave the apartment, and had been bed-ridden for many years. Alyosha never visited his father, although he lived nearby. Alyosha's mother looked after the invalid, her former husband, from whom she had been divorced a long time ago.

"I last saw him when I was twelve years old, I think," Alyosha said. "Or eleven."

It was quite unclear whether he was ashamed of this or not. I thought a little then about Alyosha, about his words and his father, but didn't come to any conclusions. I don't like to think about such things generally.

Alyosha was soon fired from his job, because he had completely stopped going there and doing anything on time; as it happened, some time later the same lot also fell to me.

I didn't see Alyosha for a long time. It seemed that he felt seriously resentful about something, but I wasn't interested in his resentment.

I still got no call from the representative office of the foreign legion.

I didn't turn the light on in the room, and rolling the black dumb-bell with my frozen-toed foot, I looked out the window, dreaming of having a smoke. I had no money to buy cigarettes.

I got the strange, inexplicable feeling that the world, which lay so firmly beneath me, was starting to strangely float away, as happens when your head spins and you feel nauseated.

Against my usual custom, unable to take it, I once went to see my neighbor, whose telephone number I had left at the representative office when I was interviewed. I asked my neighbor: "Has anyone been looking for me?"

That time no one had been looking for me, but a few days later, my neighbor knocked on my door: "There's a call for you!"

I ran across the landing barefoot, and grabbed the receiver.

"So, are you still working? Idiots like you stay afloat everywhere," I heard Alyosha's voice. He was undoubtedly drunk. "Aren't they taking you into their… what's it called? Pension… Legion… Do you miss manly work? You want to shoot someone's head off, don't you?" Alyosha laughed deliberately into the phone. "The cannibal poet… You, you, I'm talking about you… A cannibal and poet. You think it's always going to be that way?..."

"Where did you get this number from?" I asked, turning to the wall and seeing my annoyed reflection in the mirror, which hung by the door, next to the telephone.

"Should that be the first question?" Alyosha asked. "Maybe you should ask how I feel? How I'm feeding my family, my daughter…"

"I don't care about your daughter," I replied

"Of course, all you care about is your reflection in the mirror."

I hung up the phone, apologized to the neighbor, and went back to my room. I went over to the bed and haphazardly kicked at the box of letters – I hit it. The papers spilled out, some pages flew from under the bed and settled on the floor with a gentle rustle. There was no rug on the floor: just painted boards, between which coins sometimes fell when I took my pants off and laid them out. Yesterday evening I had pointlessly wiggled an iron ruler, left over from previous tenants, into a gap, and barely resisted the temptation to break one of the boards. There was a coin with the number 5 there, I thought. A packet of Korean noodles. Even two packets, if you bought the cheaper kind.

For the first time in years, I was furious.

Throwing on a light jacket, in the pocket of which several coins had clinked yesterday, or to be precise two, I went to buy bread. On the door of the small, quiet shop, there was a sign: "Loader urgently wanted."

The next evening I went to work.

Loading bread was a pleasant task. Three times a night, there was a knock on the iron shutters. *Who's there?* I was supposed to ask, but I never did, I just opened up – simply because a minute before I had heard the sound of the bread truck approaching. A gloomy driver stood on the other side of the window. He handed me a form, I signed it, the pen was always in the pocket of my grey uniform.

Then he opened up the doors of the truck, which he had backed up to the window of the shop. The truck was full of trays with bread. He gave them to me, and I ran around the shop with the trays, putting them in special stands – the white bread went with the white bread, the rye bread with the rye bread.

The bread was still warm. I bent my face over it, and every time I could hardly restrain myself from biting off an aromatic piece of it as I ran.

Once, in the morning, the driver put a tray of bread on the window before I came back. Without waiting for me, the driver went back into the truck for the next tray, and the tray that was on the window fell off. The bread scattered over the floor, and a few buns were covered in the dirt that had been tracked in by my shoes.

"What the fuck are you doing?" the driver was quick to blame me for my sluggishness, although it was his fault.

I didn't say anything: to punch him in his stupid face, I would have to walk through the shop to the exit, open the iron door with two locks on it, fumble with the long key that didn't always go in right away…

The truck shortly left, and I turned on the light in the shop, and gathered the buns off the floor. I wiped them with my sleeve, and put them back on the tray. Two pink buns wouldn't get clean – the dirt only smeared over them, so I spat on their pink sides several times – that was a much easier and better way to clean them.

Alyosha appeared by the shop quite by accident, and I still can't fathom why he was made to cross my path this time.

I was on my way to my shift, finishing a cigarette, taking the last drags and throwing the butt in the ash-bin, and Alyosha came towards me out of the open doors of my shop.

Not seeing any reason to still be angry with him, I greeted Alyosha, and even gave him a small hug.

"What, do you work here?" he asked.

"I'm a loader," I replied, smiling.

"Can I come in? To get warm? For a little while?" Alyosha asked hurriedly, clearly not wanting to hear a refusal. "I'm going home soon anyway, I've bought presents for my daughter," he showed me a bag as proof.

"No, you can't right now," I replied. "Only when the salespeople and the manager leave. In an hour."

An hour later someone started banging on the door. Alyosha was already drunk, and with a friend.

The friend, I must say, seemed to me to be a decent guy, with a childish look, healthy, taller than me, and quite charming – he had small ears on a large head, and a warm palm. He was silent almost the whole time, and did not even try to participate in the conversation, but he smiled so touchingly that I constantly wanted to shake his hand.

I showed them my bread and my trays. I took them to the little room where I'd recently been spending my boring nights, as if in expectation of some disaster, without really knowing what it looked like: since my fourth year at school, when older pupils had taken money from me, I hadn't experienced any disasters.

The guys had brought vodka with them

"There'll be warm bread coming soon," I promised.

By the time the bread was delivered, we were all drunk already, and were laughing a lot.

Alyosha was showing me the presents for his daughter. First there was a strange anemic fluffy animal that I flicked on the nose, which genuinely offended Alyosha. Then the book "*Karlsson*" with color illustrations.

"It's my favorite story," Alyosha said, unexpectedly serious. "I read it from the age of four to the age of fourteen. Several times a year."

He told me this in such a tone of voice as if he was admitting something incredibly important.

Ever since I was a child, I couldn't stand that book... I thought clearly, but did not say it out loud.

As I stomped across the stone floor to open the window where I was given bread, I remembered how Alyosha had just tenderly slapped his new friend on the shoulder, and said:

"Drink up, boy!" – and turning to me, he added: "But you're not a boy anymore." And we all laughed, without understanding what exactly we were laughing at.

A minute later, laughing, the three of us unloaded the bread together. The driver – the same one, I think – kept looking at us with interest.

As I took the last tray of bread, I swore at him for no reason. He responded – but without much ill-will, and even, immediately understanding the mood I was in, he tried to put the situation right, and said some words of reconciliation. But I had already given the tray to Alyosha's new friend, and went to open the door.

"Wait there, I'm coming out," I said to the driver over my shoulder.

On the way, I remembered that I was going to the doors without keys, I'd put the keys on the table in the little office, I thought. I went back but couldn't find them, and for some reason moved the opened bottles and bitten pieces of bread around. I found the keys in the inside pocket of my uniform – and realized that I had felt them jabbing me painfully when I pressed the tray to my chest.

When I got outside, the truck had driven off. The smell of bread drifted out of the shop into the street.

Alyosha wandered out after me with a cigarette between his teeth. Following him, smiling gently, his friend appeared in the open door.

We threw snowballs, trying to hit the streetlight, but missed – although we did hit a window, from behind which, trying to save the street lights from us, an unknown woman threatened us, banging on the glass.

Acting stupid, Alyosha's friend and I banged our shoulders together, and I suggested that we fight, not seriously, just for fun – by hitting each other with our open hands, not with our fists. He agreed.

We stood in position. I jumped energetically, while he didn't move, and looked at me almost tenderly.

I took a step forward, and was immediately knocked down by a direct blow to the head. The fist that hit me was clenched.

When I came to a minute later, I rubbed snow into my temples and forehead for a long time. The snow was hard and had no smell.

"Did you fall down?" Alyosha asked, not putting any emotion into his question.

I shook my head and squinted sideways at him: it was painful to turn my head. He was smoking, very calmly, directly in the light of the street lamp, bright from the snow.

The next day I got a call from the legion office. I told them that I wasn't going anywhere.

Wheels

...So I found myself in a cemetery.

Once I was visiting a stupid friend of mine. We were just sitting around watching television, he yearned with the desire to entertain himself somehow, and I was lying on his musty couch.

This was in a dormitory on the fifth floor.

Through the open door covered in dents and marks, came a kitten of nasty appearance, looking as if it had lived in a rubbish pail all its life.

My friend turned to it his idiotic attention.

"Hey you, shithead," he welcomed the squealing animal and picked it up, looking it over in an unfriendly way.

We had just had a smoke, spitting into the autumn damp, and the window was open.

When I turned away from the television, the kitten was already hanging from the windowsill with its paws, scraping up white patches of paint with its crooked claws. It was amazing that the animal did not make a noise as it slid toward its feline non-existence.

I remembered for no reason that some poet said that the other world smelt of mice. Our kitten would like it if that were so. But I don't think it smells of anything at all there.

My fool looked at the kitten in fascination.

A second later, the kitten suddenly clutched at an invisible crack on the window sill with its last efforts, and hung there motionless, its eyes staring.

The fool made a tiny movement with his index finger – the way you touch a bell or a shot glass if you want it to make a delicate sound – and hit the kitten on its hanging claw.

When I went down on to the street, after first calling the fool by his everlasingly true name, the kitten was lying on the bench, peaceful and soft. Its back paws hung off the bench like rags.

This is just the way that I was hit, with a light movement, on the claw.

But I did have merry friends.

Vadya, a handsome, smiling blonde guy, his eyes with the ruptured veins of a novice but already incorrigible alcoholic. Vova, the healthiest of us, chuckling, meaty, with a large red face.

It was the most poetic winter I have ever experienced in my life.

At that time I had finally stopped writing poems, and never did so again seriously, I quit one job but did not find another one, and then, as I say, I was hit on the claw, and I found myself in a grave.

"Are you going to get out of there, monkey dick?" Vova called, standing above me. From under his feet, earth and dirty snow fell into the grave.

I grabbed the spade, and swung it with the genuine intention of hitting Vovka on the leg as painfully as possible, and if possible breaking it.

Vovka, laughing, jumped away. In one hand he had a bottle of vodka, in the other a glass.

"No, are you going to drink or not?" he asked, walking around the grave, keeping his distance from my spade.

"Why the fuck are you asking, Vova?"

"Then get out."

"I'll drink here."

Vova, making sure that I had put the spade in the corner, squatted by the rectangular pit. He handed me a tall glass, half filled.

Next to Vova, Vadik squatted down, smiling his usual sincere, kind smile.

We clinked our glasses – the guys had to lean over towards me a little, and I raised my glass towards them, as if greeting them.

I stood without a hat, sweaty, happy, in a black, or rather red, pit, dug out in the midst of white snow. The snow lay on faint paths, on statues and on iron fences, on graves and on disheveled wreaths.

Vova handed me a piece of bread and a slice of sausage.

How delicious, my God. Cover me over right now, I know what happiness is.

Vova turned around to bring more snacks, and got the scoop of the spade in his backside.

"Damn you, earthworm!" he shouted happily, and didn't do anything to retaliate.

Vadik also laughed. White unchewed bread could be seen in his mouth, and this seemed attractive to me. Vadik had good, strong, white teeth – and now there was white bread in his teeth.

"Let's finish up now, we'll get the coffin," Vova said. "Who have we got today? An old woman?"

Making mournful faces, we entered the apartment.

Already on our way to the fourth floor, we had stopped talking, in order to calm down somehow. Otherwise the corpse would have been collected by three sweaty guys who had drunk two bottles of vodka between them, with teeth chattering, and with a stupid chuckle bubbling in their teeth.

Quiet relatives moved aimlessly along the walls, women in black scarfs and men in coats. At loose ends, the men went out to smoke in the stairwell every ten minutes.

"Time to take her away?" they asked, as if we were in charge in this home.

"Yes," I replied.

"Need any help?"

"No, we're fine."

Until recently I had only carried cupboards up and down staircases. Now I had realized that a coffin was essentially no different from furniture. You just couldn't turn it upside down.

Vova always went first, and carried the narrow end, the legs. Vadya and I clung on at the back.

We were slowly followed by a few friends or relatives. Their somber faces reflected the conviction that any minute we would drop the coffin.

But we completed our task energetically, and almost easily.

By the entrance, we put the coffin on some stools. We all took a breather.

"Could you take a photo of Grandma?" someone asked me.

"Sure," I replied, before I could get my breath back, surprised as usual at why the hell people needed pictures of corpses. Where did they put them, did they hang them on the wall? *Look, kids, that's your grandma.* Or did they put the photo in an album? *That's us at the beach, there we are at our neighbors' dacha, and this is the funeral... It's not a good photo of me, don't look.*

I put the instant photo in my pocket so that it would come out without being affected by the winter sun and light snow.

The bus drove up, and the driver got out, and opened the back doors of his rust heap.

The relatives had all wandered off somewhere, even the one who asked me to take a photo.

"All right, load it in," said the driver.

Vadya shrugged his shoulders: he was smiling again.

"Listen, let's load it in while there's no one around," Vova said to me. "My legs are freezing. Otherwise they'll come out and start milling around."

And indeed, the relatives did not come out to say goodbye until quarter of an hour later, and Grandma was already on the bus.

By that time we'd already managed to argue with the driver, asking him to turn the heater on; he looked at us as if we were idiots and didn't turn it on.

"Don't be sad, granny, we're about to go," I said quite seriously, but my silly brothers, who were stomping their frozen legs in boots that were rock-hard from frost, found this incredibly funny.

"What, aren't we allowed to say goodbye?" a tearful woman's voice said. The door opened after the voice, and we saw a small crying face, which was hardly visible under black lace, so abundant that it was almost indecent.

"Shall we carry her out again?" Vova asked insolently.

"Never mind now…" the woman replied.

A man came bounding up to us, evidently very happy that we weren't taking the coffin out.

"Are you cold, guys?" he asked affably.

"Are we ever…"

Something that I can never understand is speeches by a grave. You stand with a spade and go crazy: you feel like knocking down the idiot who's talking, so that he spills, the asshole, into the red pit. It's embarrassing to listen to people, where does all this stupidity in them come from?

Nailing down the coffin lids with long, reliable nails is also something that I don't like doing very much, for some reason; but this is probably because I can't do it as nimbly as Vova. He drives the nail in with three blows – beautiful work…

Lowering the coffin is much more interesting: it has a bit of a children's game to it, a painstaking, pointless child's task. One of the men who has come to pay his respects always helps us out here: because we need four, not three men.

And shoveling in the earth is quite enjoyable… We take off our jackets, cheerful, continuous sweat runs down our handsome faces, and the spades fly. First the earth falls loudly, hitting the wood, then it falls with a dull thud. The sound gets duller and duller. And then just a soft hill is left, and we have made all our morning's work on the frozen earth come to nothing.

Now there's time to have a good smoke, while the rest slowly disperse. We smoke, licking the frozen salty moisture from our lips. Now we will be taken to the wake, at some shabby café, and we'll get drunk.

We're always happy when we are seated somewhere in the corner, or better still, at a separate table.

I like cheap cafés, their damp smell, as if they cooked soup there around the clock, and swimming in the soup are tired vegetables, withered potatoes, exhausted carrots, and among other things, it seems, the cook's apron, if not in its entirety, then at least the pocket…

In cheap cafés, there are dark windows, with mist-covered glazed tiles, and dirty windowsills. When you move the chairs, they make a horrible squeak as they move across the broken square tiles, and the tables shake, drenching themselves with juice. We have juice on the table, I don't like it, but I'll drink it.

Initially we behave quietly, we eat everything quickly, and so they start to serve the new dishes with our table. It is always empty, our table, in two minutes there is not even any mustard on it, Vova has scraped out the jar with his heavy, chapped fingers; only the lumpy grey salt remains in the salt cellar. We'd sprinkle the salt on some bread, but we already ate the bread, before we had hardly sat down.

After half an hour, the wake gets noisy, and no one hears or sees us anymore. Sometimes someone may sit down with us and say that grandma was a good person. And we drink with him without clinking our glasses, although he is eager to bash his glass against ours. He's not used to it yet, perhaps this is his first grandma, but we've had so many, we don't even remember which number this one is.

Vova, the cunning bastard, has gone to take a leak, and has already found out where the crates of vodka are, two of them, and snatches a bottle without asking – they take a long time to bring us one, and there is still a lot of food, we're used to consuming it sparingly.

As soon as we realize that the relatives have already begun to thin out, and our young, undesirably cheerful voices sound too loud in the emptying café, we guess that we should leave.

We swallow the food, stick an unfinished pie in our pockets, and pour out the new bottle, almost a whole glass each, gulp it down and rush outside, to cool off our hot heads.

We smoke and jostle each other, and look at each other tenderly. No one wants to go home, and waits for events to take some interesting turn of their own accord.

"Shall we go home or what?" asks Vova, and I hear cunning in his voice.

"I don't really feel like it yet," Vadya replies, showing his white teeth, like a friendly horse.

And here Vova takes out a bottle from under his arm.

"You stole it, you bastard!" I say, laughing. "You robbed an old woman, student!"

"Student yourself," Vova replies cheerfully; his words are not lacking in respect. In our group I am considered to be the smartest, although I have the same education: a tedious school and Cs on my report.

We need to find a place for ourselves, and we start our circling around the town, feeling the dampness in our legs and the icy drafts less and less, opening our collars, pulling up our hats, catching snow in our mouths.

We don't find the casually menitoned friend of Vova or Vadya at home; it's unlikely he would have been happy to see us, but he would have taken us in for an hour; Vadya or Vova's aunt sent us away without opening the door; and the skanky girlfriend of both Vadya and Vova turned out to have left town.

"Where to?" we ask at the peephole.

"To her village," the man behind the door replies. "She was expelled from the institute because of studs like you."

After saying this he flapped off in his slippers, back into the depths of the apartment, without saying goodbye.

Vova rang the doorbell again, and getting a reply, pressed his red face against the peep-hole.

"Stud yourself," Vova said clearly.

It didn't seem likely that anyone else was waiting for us in this town, and so we settled on the steps of the stairwell, squatting down in a circle: the freezing concrete of the steps was intolerable, even if you wrapped a jacket around your ass.

Vova produced a piece of sausage from out of his coat, and a third of a stick of bread, and a loaf evenly cut in two.

My spirits rose again, and my heart started racing.

In a hurry, we drank, passing the bottle around, and tore the bread in pieces, chewing on the sausage meat in turn. The pie that we had brought from the wake proved to be useful.

We laughed, interrupting each other with every kind of heresy, that was quite worthy of the walls of this stairwell.

A key turned in an iron lock, and the man who had talked to Vova came out.

Vova was sitting with his back to him and didn't turn around – at that moment he was drinking out of the bottle, and never allowed himself to be distracted from this activity.

"Maybe you'd like a mug?" the man asked.

"Bring us something to wash it down with," Vova asked hoarsely, lowering the bottle, but without turning around.

I had been drinking for the fourth month now, and I drank every day.

At home – the place where I resided – lived my mother and my sister, who was divorced and had a small child.

I didn't get up in the morning, to avoid running into my mother, who was hurrying off to work. She always left breakfast for me, but I didn't eat it. I can't eat in the morning when I have a hangover.

Lying on the bed, gloomy, feeling as though my head had been squashed, I ran my hands over the bed and noticed that there was no sheet on it. And the blanket had no blanket cover.

"Pissed myself again..."

Screwing up my eyes from the vile sense of shame that made my brain go into spasms, I remembered how my mother and sister had turned me over at night, taking the sheet out from under me. And then, with a gentle movement, they had covered my drunken body with another blanket, instead of the wet one.

After lying there for an hour or so, I went out of my room, saw my sister breastfeeding her baby, and quickly hid in the bathroom. I didn't wash there, no, I cleaned my teeth, looking at myself in the mirror, with hatred, but not without curiosity.

So that's what you can do, I wanted to say. *And it's nothing to you... Everything is nothing to you.*

It started in December, which was unusually lacking in snow. After the first abundant, wet November snow fell, everything quieted down and melted, the roads turned black again and revolting bushes stuck out, scrawny and bent out of shape with loathing for themselves. In the morning, the puddles were covered with a crust of ice, but there was no snow.

I remember that my sister was still walking the baby in a pram, dressing him in a hundred layers of clothing and wrapping him in three blankets. He lay there, not even able to wrinkle his nose, and breathed in the brittle snowless frost.

Once I took the pram into the stairwell, without the baby, whom my sister was dressing despite his dissatisfied grunting.

After I pressed the button for the lift, I remembered that I had left the pacifier in the apartment, although my sister had just mentioned it.

I went back into the apartment, took the rubber nipple from off the bed, and as I went back into the stairwell, I saw that a man I didn't know was leaning out of the open door of the lift and briskly rifling through our pram. He was going through the diapers, digging among the pillows and grazing the offended rattles.

"What are you doing, asshole?" I asked in a surprised voice.

"Why did you leave it here?" he replied, snarling with grey teeth.

As I ran to the lift, I noticed that he wasn't alone in the lift – next to him, evidently, was his wife, and behind him was his daughter, around nine years old, with dull eyes.

He pressed the button, and the lift went up.

With angry leaps I flew up the stairs, and pressing my face to the doors of the lift, I yelled:

"Where do you maggots come from?!"

I saw the cable moving past in the gap in the lift; there was a faint yellow light. The lift didn't stop.

I ran up another two floors, hoping to overtake it. I flew to the lift but missed it again: the lift went higher, although I had just clearly heard it stopping with a clatter.

"Why are you alive, you piece of crap?" I shouted into the doors of the lift.

Thus, screaming on every floor and tearing up my throat, I ran up to the ninth floor, sat down on the stairs there and cried, but without tears: I drily howled in my heavy melancholy. The lift went down.

I went back down in about seven minutes, with a cigarette between my teeth. My sister was putting the baby in the pram.

"Where did you go?" she asked.

I didn't answer. I pressed the button of the lift again.

We wheeled the pram out and went off for a walk.

As I looked at the baby, I noticed something on his cheerful red hat.

I leant down and saw that it was a thick, disgusting, pink blob of spit that had spread on the pillow.

The man had gone to the trouble of stopping the lift on the second floor and spitting into the pram.

I rubbed it off with my hand.

As we finished the bottle of vodka, we started doing what we usually did: we collected change and the crumpled, almost worthless notes in our pockets. We put all the money on the step.

This was one of our personal, almost daily repeating miracles – somehow we, who thought that we had no money at all, after shaking ourselves down to the last kopeck, put together just enough to buy a bottle every time. And we even had a few rubles left over for the cheapest and nastiest rusks.

We had our norm, and we did not usually part until we had fulfilled it. The norm was three bottles per person. The three of us had to drink nine bottles by midnight, or a little later. And only after that did we start to go our separate ways, no longer having any words for farewells or energy for friendly hugs.

Today – still rather sober and much happier than we had been an hour ago – we drank... we gathered our efforts and counted... yes, we had only drunk six bottles.

Two while we were digging the grave. Three at the wake. And another in the stairwell.

So we put together money for the seventh and went out to look for it.

We found a shop and bought everything there that we wanted. The vodka disappeared into Vova's shapeless jacket, and I put the rusks in my pocket, feeling their roughness with my fingers.

"I don't want to drink outside anymore," I said with capricious sternness.

"Who does?" Vova replied. "What can you suggest?"

I didn't have any suggestions, and for a while we walked silently, gradually losing the warmth we had accumulated in the stairwell, where at least there wasn't any wind.

"Hey, a girl I went to school with lived around here somewhere," Vova suddenly livened up.

"When did you go to school, weirdo?" I asked.

Vova didn't say anything in reply, and looked at the buildings. They stood in freezing semi-darkness, with their grey sides turned towards each other, completely identical.

Despite the cold, the vodka we had drunk in the stairwell was slowly reaching us: but the drunkenness did not bring joy anymore, it had to be carried, like an extra burden, along with the cold and the darkness.

It was impossible to believe that anything could be good anymore: that warmth and light existed; you miserably wanted to lie down somewhere. But you didn't want to go home, where you would be watched with suffering eyes.

Vova led us through yards, hunched over, silent, with our heads tucked into our jackets; our black hats were pulled down to our noses.

Vova himself didn't care, he was still carrying his red face high and cheerfully.

"That's it!" he exclaimed. "Here!"

And he guessed right. The door was opened by a small, dark, but already grown-up girl, and, which we did not expect at all, she smiled to us in welcome.

Vova called her something, but I didn't catch what exactly, I just barged into the apartment and noticed right away that there was a delicious smell.

In fact, it wasn't anything special – it was just hot borshch steaming in the kitchen. When you come in from the cold, a pot of red borshch quite rightly seems to be an aromatic miracle, or even something divine. There's something pagan about it...

We took off our coats, moving our rigid hands with difficulty, pulled off our frozen footwear and went into the big room, where some guy was sitting. When he saw us, he immediately started preparing to leave, and no one asked him to stay.

Vova, evidently, wasn't embarrassed by anything. He didn't care that we had turned up uninvited, made ourselves at home and hadn't brought anything with us.

What do you mean, we didn't bring anything, Vova would have reasoned, if he had been capable. *We've got vodka.*

He went to get the bottle, which was still concealed in his jacket (he didn't produce it until the guy we didn't know had gone) and showed the vodka to the girl.

"Will you drink with us?" Vova offered, smiling insolently.

"I'll be glad to join you," she replied with unusual kindness, and I immediately wanted to do something useful for her, so that she would remember it all her life.

"Would you like some borshch?" she asked, shifting her gaze from Vova to me, but as I couldn't reply, she had to return her gaze to Vova.

"Certainly!" he said confidently.

The girl went out, and we heard the clink of bowls being placed on the table.

"Why are you so lugubrious?" Vova asked me.

"What?"

"Lugubrious."

"What does that mean?"

"Melancholy. Sour. Down in the dumps."

I was always prepared to like a person for even the smallest act, if it was an honest one. And even for saying a word that hit the nail on the head. I had respected Vova for a long time, but here he defined the way I felt so wonderfully that the warm feeling I felt for him suddenly transformed into a full sensation of life-long kinship.

You're right, Vova, I'm not sad at all. And not even tired. I'm lugubrious, with hanging, weak-willed cheeks, soft lips and sleepy eyelids.

Immediately, I felt happy again, and we went to eat and drink. The first spoon of borshch gave me back the taste of happiness, full and persistent.

After the second shot of vodka, we forgot about Vova's classmate and made jokes among ourselves. We could never remember what made us happy in those minutes, especially as we weren't really capable of associating with each other when we were sober: until the first burning gulp we couldn't find a single thing to talk about.

She sat a little distance from the table, and slowly ate our rusks, which I had handed her ceremoniously.

Unobtrusive music was playing, and Vova's classmate sometimes wagged her small chin in rhythm with the music. She was not attractive at all, but this did not prevent her from being a wonderful person who had taken us in and wasn't making us go away.

By the time the bottle was almost empty I felt that I was getting drunk again, and I went to look at myself in the bathroom, and also to rinse my face with icy water: that sometimes helped.

I couldn't find the light switch, so I left the door open, turned on the tap, poured water into my cupped hand and presssed it to my face. I bent down over the sink.

A little light came from the corridor, and I looked around. The reflections in the dark mirror were hard to decipher, but I did notice that the bar to which the shower curtain was attached was hanging crookedly.

I'll fix everything for you, my dear, I thought tenderly. *I should ask for a screwdriver, it's probably all screwed together... I'll just have a look how it's attached and... I'll ask for a screwdriver...*

Holding on to the shower curtain, I stood on the edge of the bath. Balancing on one leg, I tried to stand up straight, but the bar didn't hold my weight, and came crashing down.

I fell off the edge of the bath, managing to grab the iron pipe of the bar before it could hit me on the head. At the same time, with a horrible swishing and rustling, I was covered in the shower curtain.

There I stood in the middle of the bathroom... with the rail in my hand... with my head wrapped in a shower curtain, like a person sheltering from a downpour...

Or perhaps it began earlier. I was returning to my suburb from the big city, the train whistled and sped through the evening drizzle, which was half snow. The moisture stuck to the windows in zigzags.

As I got out of the train, I stood on the platform for a long time, feeding on the gusts of wind, as if hoping that they would blow away all of my unexpected feebleness.

Recently I had got a feeling that was similar to the damp growing pains of boys going through puberty.

Strangely enough, in my early youth, having lived on earth for one and a half decades, I quickly passed these growing pains. The distance between a suddenly ending childhood to the moment when the most beautiful girl at school began to talk to me was imperceptible and laughable. I didn't remember this distance.

And so, I virtually did not experience the humiliation felt by all my peers, which arose from the incompatibility of their bulging desires and the awkward opportunities of realizing them.

But now I felt as if teenage apathy and inarticulateness had taken control of me.

Some awkward wind blew me to the building on the outskirts where my girlfriend from school lived, who, I say, was very beautiful, and whom I never loved.

I got there by a feeble trolleybus, in an empty cabin, with just me and the conductor, and I squatted in the stuffy stairwell, under the staircase on the first floor, remembering without any enthusiasm how here I had first touched a vagina, and how the hairs on it had seemed incredibly bristly to me.

I remembered how we dragged our schoolbags, moving from one floor to the next to avoid the ubiquitous lift, which opened with a clatter and poured out noisy people into the stairwell.

Why am I remembering that? I thought without irritation.

Sometimes people came out of the stairwell and didn't notice me, and this seemed humiliating.

Then I had a smoke, slowly inhaling the smoke and examining at the cigarette. This is the way people look when they have only recently discovered tobacco.

I was naïve enough to believe that the spirits of my youth were still alive in the stairwell, and I was pleased that I was indifferent to them, and that they were probably also indifferent to me, perhaps they didn't even recognize me, just sniffed me over and flew away.

Neither was I recognized by a large dog, which was being taken for a walk by a sullen-looking person. They entered the stairwell, bringing into its musty silence the damp smell of the street, the noise of clothes, the banging and squeaking of doors. The dog immediately saw me and lunged at my legs. Thankfully, it was on a leash.

It barked emphatically, right at my face, stretching out its neck, and it did not seem as if its master was making much effort to restrain his furious monster.

"Call off your dog! Call it off!" I shouted. "It's going to bite my head off!"

I pressed my head against the wall and felt the stench of the dog's snout, saw the roof of its mouth and its wet tongue.

The man was in no hurry and deliberately pulled the dog towards himself slowly. The dog struggled and sprayed spit.

"You're sick!" I shouted, shielding myself with my sleeve.

"Get out of the building," he replied. "Go away, you tramp!"

Holding the dog on the leash and showing that he was prepared to release it, the man waited for me to get up and go out.

He shouted after me, but his words were inaudible over the barking.

Not without horror, I imagined that I had carelessly torn the rail out of the wall, and now, above the bathroom tiles, there would be two gaping holes in the crumbling plaster and whitewash.

What will I say to Vova's classmate? What have I done!

Somehow freeing myself from the shower curtain, I looked at the place where the rail had just been, and with a feel of incredible relief realized that nothing terrible had happened.

The rail had been fixed on plastic hooks, one of which had simply turned over, thus making the iron pipe fall on me, together with the shower curtain that was attached to it.

I put the rail in its place and went out of the bathroom. No one had heard anything.

Vova was asking his classmate for a loan, but she replied that she did not have any money.

I didn't have the energy to talk. I sat at the table in silence, completely stupefied.

In the bowl, with red froth around the edges, lay a leaf of boiled cabbage.

My friends started getting ready to go, but I couldn't pull myself together to stand up.

"Hey, cripple, get up!" Vova called to me after a few minutes.

His classmate started taking away the dishes.

For some reason I wanted to tell her that my friends and I had not been with any women for a long time, almost three months. And before that I hadn't been with a woman for a long time either, perhaps a whole month in addition to that. But back then I still remembered them, and now I had completely forgotten all about them, and I felt much better.

We never talk about women and never pay attention to them if we're walking along the street. We're always going somewhere.

But I didn't talk about that, having remembered another story, which was very touching. How once, this winter, at the very beginning of it, I left the apartment building and saw a little girl on the swings.

I wanted to push her on the swings. This is what I said, looking into the bowl and enunciating the words with intolerable difficulty: "I… wanted… so… much… to… push… her… and she replied…"

She replied:

"Don't touch me. You're ugly."

After I said that, I finally got up and went to put my coat on. I took a long time to pull on my shoes, listening to the splash of water and the sound of dishes being put away in the cupboard.

Then I searched for the arms of my jacket, for some reason finding only one arm, or three at once. The guys were already smoking in the stairwell, waiting for me.

After she had washed the dishes, she went to close the door after me, but I didn't go out, and silently looked in her face, which I couldn't make out, and would never remember later if I wanted to.

"I'll give you my phone number, and you can ring me," I said firmly, feeling as if I was going to be sick.

She shrugged her shoulders, tired.

I fished around in my pocket and took out a firm, square piece of paper.

"Give me…a feltpen… I'll write it down."

She took a pencil from the table by the mirror and gave it to me.

I wet the pencil with my saliva and wrote down the number, realizing that I had forgotten it somewhat and had probably got three numbers wrong out of six.

"There," I gave her the square with crooked numbers on it.

"What is this?" she said in disgust.

On the other side of the telephone number there was the instant photo of the dead old woman. The woman's lips were firmly closed. You could clearly see her brown eyelids and her white sunken cheeks.

"How disgusting," said the girl in revulsion. "Where did you get that from? Why do you carry it in your pocket? You're mad. Take it away!"

I don't know where we found money again: I think we came across it after a fight by a kiosk at night.

I remember that Vova, endowed with incredible strength, knocked down two guys, grabbing them by the collar and throwing them onto the asphalt as if they were completely helpless.

We drank vodka in an underpass, and our hoarse lalughter was continued by a distorting, broken echo.

Vadya had disappeared somewhere, and Vova and I drank almost the entire bottle together. We only had a tiny toffee to eat as a snack, which I found in my pocket, covered in specks of tobacco and fluff – from the lining.

I bit the toffee in two and gave the other half to Vova. As we swallowed the vodka, we would nibble a tiny piece of the sweet, crunching it between our teeth and grimacing.

"Vova, have you ever thought... that every year... you live out the day of your death?" I asked. "Perhaps it's today? We live it out every year... Vova!"

Vova shook his head, not understanding a word I said.

Then Vadya came back, and we drank some more, but I just had a little bit. I took a few gulps into my mouth and spat almost everything out.

I went outside and soaked the iron wall of the kiosk with steaming urine. As I did up my pants, I saw a woman crouching nearby. She got up, pulled her pants on and returned to the kiosk, closing the heavy door behind her. We weren't at all surprised by each other's presence.

Forgetting about my friends, I wandered off home. I had no money for a taxi, the trams weren't running at this hour, and I walked along, barely aware of where I was going, only sometimes coming to my senses and recognizing familiar objects in my part of town.

My path home went across the railroad tracks. I still don't remember how many of them there are, three or four: they're smooth, heavy rails, which come together and then diverge.

At one place on the rails, there was a battered crossing platform.

As I walked towards the tracks, I heard the rumble of an approaching train, a freight train. Sometimes I'd get the idea of counting the wagons of freight trains, but once I reached fifty I got tired.

Unless I cross the tracks now, I'll fall down before it's gone by, it's heavy and long… I'll fall down here and freeze! I realized, without saying this, and gathering my strength, I ran.

The rumble was getting nearer.

Tripping over the rails, not finding the platform, I ran diagonally, sensing the approaching iron mass, the burning smell and the heat.

In my right pupil, a lamp with a long white light was reflected.

My foot slipped, and I fell on my side, on to the gravel bank, and immediately, at that very second, I saw the black shining wheels steaking past with a terrible roar.

I gathered gravel in my palm, I felt the gravel with my cheek, and for a few minutes I couldn't breathe: the huge wheels burnt the air, leaving a feeling of hot, stifling, mad emptiness.

Six cigarettes and so on

By his hands I could tell that he wasn't my enemy.

So I relaxed immediately.

He entered loudly, clinking the keys on his finger, the poser.

I looked out the window: sure enough, outside under the quiet rain falling from above, in the light of the street lamps, his long car was parked, pretty as a fish.

He spoke rudely to the barman with the nasty voice of an old pederast, sat on a tall stool opposite the bar, loudly moved the ashtray closer and threw the cigarette packet on to the table. A poser, as I said. He was wearing an overcoat.

"Are you asleep, you big-mouthed shmuck? The work day hasn't started yet, and you're already asleep. Give me a lighter, how long do I have to suck on an unlit cigarette?"

The barman Vadik extended him a lighter.

The poser took a few seconds to light up, looking at Vadik, and deliberately keeping the cigarette away from the flame. Vadik moved the lighter towards him, and the poser moved his head, mockingly moving his fat lips holding the filter.

It's my conviction that people like this should be killed immediately, and that no one should ever regret it.

But I'm the bouncer here, I get paid for doing other things.

I'm not even obliged to protect Vadik. Barmen are crooks, at the end of the night there's bound to be a scandal: one of the customers will discover that they have been charged for several dishes that nobody ordered.

I'm surprised that barmen don't get beaten up: customers prefer to beat each other up, and break the dishes.

Although I feel sorry for Vadik now.

"Why aren't there any girls here?" the poser asked, finally lighting up.

Vadik mumbled something in reply, to the effect that it was probably too early in the day.

"Maybe I should screw you, how about that?"

The barman rubbed the glasses, not replying.

The poser smiled, not taking his eyes off Vadik. I saw all of this from the store room, where I was tying my shoelaces.

It really gets me down to see men acting incapably like this: poor Vadik, how does he live if this is what he's like. He's taller than I am, and of average build. He's a pale, quite charming guy.

He has a girlfriend, quite striking, she sometimes turns up before the club opens, and reads a textbook – she's a student. Vadik pours her some coffee, and she drinks it neatly, not tearing her eyes away from the page. If she could hear this now, if only she could see it.

No one prohibits Vadik from saying something insulting to the poser, to call him a mud toad, a fat-lipped scumbag.

And if the poser tries to hit the barman, then I will have to intervene.

But Vadik just keeps furiously rubbing the glasses.

I tied my shoelaces and came out, and sat on a stool at the bar, next to the poser.

And here I realized that he was not my enemy. His fingers were puffy and pink; his fist was feeble and soft, like a frog's belly, he hadn't hit anyone with this hand for a long time.

"What are you carrying on for?" I asked, looking at him.

He didn't show any sign of alarm, of course – he reacted to me calmly.

"It's all OK, we're just talking. Right, Vadim?"

The barman had his name written on a tag attached to his shirt.

Vadik nodded.

"Can I get you a beer?" the poser offered.

"Sure," I said.

I wasn't allowed to drink at work, but the owner hadn't turned up yet. Also, I drink a bit every night anyway, and pretend to hide this from the owner – and the owner, in his turn, pretends that he doesn't notice how badly, without inspiration, I hide this from him.

Vadik poured me a beer, and with pleasure I drank almost the whole glass in one gulp.

Sometimes I swear not to drink at the customers' expense, so as not to get close to them, but every time I break my word.

Now the poser will start talking to me. He'll start probing with his fingernail, half-joking, half-insulting, and see what reaction he gets: it's the usual habit of a lowlife – to find out who you're dealing with.

"Where were you hiding when I came in?" he asked.

"I didn't see you. You're not noticeable," I replied, got up, and pushing away the glass, went to my usual spot.

It's a wooden counter by the entrance to the club; to the left is a glass door that leads outside, to the right is a glass door to the club. There are two tall stools by the counter. I sit at one of them, Zakhar is my name, and my partner sits on the other, he's called Syoma, but I call him Molotok, Hammer, because he has the wonderful surname Molotilov.

Unlike me, he doesn't smoke and never drinks alcohol. He's also about forty kilograms heavier than me. He knows how to hit a person in the chest, say, or in the abdomen so that it makes a noise like hitting a pillow. A dull but juicy "boom!" I can't do that.

I'm sure that Molotok is stronger than I am, but for some reason he considers me to be the one in charge.

He's always in a good mood.

He came in with his usual smile, out of the evening cold after the rain, with his jacket swishing, stamping his boots, a great, reliable guy, with a handshake with a pressure of four atmospheres, and a bag of sandwiches over his shoulder. He needs constant nourishment.

And he himself is designed simply and honestly, like a good sandwich, without any distracting thoughts or any melancholy. The conversation will start with the fact that it's gotten colder outside, then he'll ask whether Lev Borisych, the owner of the club, has arrived, then he'll tell me how much weight he lifted today in the bench press.

"Who's that jerk sitting there?" Syoma asked, nodding towards the poser.

I shrugged. I didn't feel like telling him about Vadik.

The first customers started to arrive. Businesslike young guys, stern pale girls: the usual night-time crowd, everyone still sober and quite respectable.

It's unlikely that any one of them can seriously upset us. Young people wear too firm an expression of confidence on their faces – but this is what reassured us. To get the better of them, all you had to do was to make their confidence waver for a second.

In general, you need to work extremely quickly and aggressively here. A fight starts with an abrupt noise: something falls down loudly, a table, a chair, dishes, sometimes everything at once. We react to noise. Syoma always works silently, I may sometimes shout angrily, *Everyone sit down!* for example, although sitting is not necessary at all, and perhaps it's even better to stand.

We single out the loudest – and throw them out the door.

These seconds on the way from the scene of the fight to the door are the most important in our job. Here a ferocious onslaught is indispensable. The person has to understand that he's literally been carried out of the café – and hasn't been hit once. He loses confidence, but doesn't have time to get angry. If we hit him, then he will have the right to get angry, and try to hit us in response. Getting into a fight with the customers is vulgar dilettantism. We try not to do this, although we're not always successful, of course.

I've heard that in neighboring clubs there have been situations when angry drunken groups beat up the security, and threw the bouncers out on the street with their faces smashed. I'd be very unhappy if something like that happened to me.

But you've got to admit that there's nothing unusual about this: for every bouncer there'll always be some animal that is stronger and more persistent; especially if there are several of these animals.

But there are just two of us, Molotok and I. For a club like this, four bouncers wouldn't be enough, but Lev Borisych, who as I already said is the owner, is incomparably economical.

The young people showed us their tickets – blue strips of paper with a stamp and price on them. Syoma cocked a cheerful eye at the girls.

As always, Lev Borisych entered swiftly, carrying his enormous stomach past us lightly; he nodded to us, barely noticeably, without opening his mouth for a greeting.

Molotok greeted him, but without any sign of servility – he's just friendly in general.

I didn't say anything, I didn't even nod in response. Lev Borisych passes by so quickly, that I could quite easily say hello to him when he can no longer see me, as he opens the door to the club. Let him think that that's the way things are: the heavy glass door has long been swinging before me, barely dispelling the thick scent of the owner's eau de cologne, and I'm still saying "…ello… ysovich!.."

I have no idea why he's in such a hurry. He's going to sit in his office with a cup of coffee all night, occasionally going to the ticket seller's office, counting the earnings and looking out into the street to see if there are any new customers. Does he really need to be in such a hurry for such important activities?

Sometimes Lev Borisych comes out into the club, trying to be as inconspicuous as possible, and if a fight breaks out, he vanishes very quickly. But he knows about everything that happens at the club, for example, how many mugs of beer I drink a night, or how much the barmen steal over the same period of time – and he does not fire the barmen every day, because new barmen will also steal. However, the staff still changes constantly, only Molotok and me are left alone. Perhaps because we're not particularly worried about keeping this job, and perhaps because we've never screwed up.

I've been inhabiting a nightclub for so long that I've forgotten about the existence of other people, besides our customers, taxi drivers, a few gangsters, a few dozen idiots pretending to be gangsters, prostitutes and mere sluts.

Although I see all these people every night, I have no idea what they do, or where their money comes from. Well, it's more or less clear with the prostitutes and taxi drivers, but what about the rest? I work here every day, but I would never come here to drink: you could spend as much at the club in fifteen minutes as I could live on for a week. If they took me on, these generous people, I would protect them for an additional payment, I don't care. Neither does Syoma. What do we care about you.

But they often care about us. Many of them think that a bouncer was created so that they could measure his strength and stupidity against theirs. The main thing is to get seriously wasted and then come to us in the foyer: *What are you looking like that for? Want to throw me out? I'm with friends...*

But even they are not the most problematic clients, of course.

There could be problems with the people who just walked past Molotok and me, for instance.

Five guys, and they just went through the door sideways, with big shoulders, big arms, and a heavy calm on their faces. They didn't even notice us – that always makes us tense.

They were dressed in jackets and light sweaters – and, as I said, they had big shoulders. I have big shoulders too, but I'm wearing two sweaters and padding, hence the shoulders. Molotok is larger, of course, but he can't compete with them either. He's not even embarrassed to admit this:

"Did you see that?"

And he shakes his head.

Molotok, of course, isn't scared, and he will stand to the end, if he has to. But his chances are zero.

Molotok and I call them "serious people."

They'll never get disgracefully drunk. They sit at a long table partitioned off by a heavy screen, in the corner of the club, away from the dance floor. They talk unhurriedly, and sometimes laugh. Lev Borysich walks around them. They called him over, quite affably. Lev Borysich sat down on the edge of a bench, like a compressed balloon – just waiting for a chance to fly away. And he did, as soon as they turned away from him, mumbling something vague about things to do or a phone call: someone was supposed to call him. At three in the morning, sure.

They rarely come here, once a month probably, and every time I'm surprised at how tangibly you can feel a real human power emanating from them.

And they don't pay attention to the women, I noticed, watching them take their habitual seats behind the screen, moving the table as if they were at home.

They don't pay attention because they're not interested in women, but because they already have women, any women they want.

They gave the vase of flowers that was on the table to the waitress who came over to them, and didn't even say: *Take it away* – she worked it out for herself, after standing for a moment with the vase in her hands.

In the dance room, the music started blaring. The first pair of young people went in, indecisively, like people entering water.

That's OK, in half an hour everyone will relax.

Sometimes, as morning approaches, I go into the dance room, and quite stupefied, I look at these ruddy people in motion. I get a feeling like you do in childhood, when you're hot and frantic, and you've been storming a snowy slope for five hours in a row, and suddenly you fall out of the game and look at everyone for a minute in surprise and think: who are we? why are we making all this noise? why is there a ringing noise in my head?

How strangely these people behave, I think, tired, in my morning mood, sleepy, looking at all the backs, heads, legs and hands. *They're adults, why are they waving their arms around like this, it's so stupid...*

But the next day I go to work again, and this feeling is almost forgotten. If I remember it, I don't understand it, I can't feel it.

"The boss wants to see you," Lev Borisych's secretary said to me, having stuck her bird-like, dark, small head with its bright lips between the glass doors.

Lev Borisych has never wanted to see me before.

"What's this about?" I asked Molotok cheerfully.

He made an uncomprehending face. We both thought that we had probably been fined. But we couldn't quite work out when this had happened.

I leapt off the stool, pushed the door, and saw Lev Borisych coming towards me and waving his hand: stay, I'll be there shortly.

"Outside, let's talk outside," he said quietly; he has the habit of repeating every phrase twice, as if testing its weight: whether he gave it away too lightly or cheaply.

We went out, and walked for a few seconds in silence, away from the club doors, and the people smoking by the entrance. I glanced sideways at Lev Borisych's stomach: *Doesn't he get cold, just wearing a shirt…* I thought.

"Can I rely on your confidentiality, Zakhar? On the confidentiality of our conversation?"

"Of course," I said, trying to say this very seriously, and even sincerely.

"Good, good… We work together, I see how you work. I'm happy with your work, I'm happy with it. There are a few little things… little things… But essentially I'm happy…" Lev Borisych said all of this quickly, looking away from me, into the bushes, at the asphalt, very attentively, as though hoping to find a coin that someone had dropped. "And we want to expand… The time has come, there are possibilities. Red light, you understand? A red light, that's what we'll have here. I'd like you to be the head of security. You understand, there can be all kinds of... excesses… excesses. Right?"

Now he looked at me for the first time, briefly and attentively.

"I agree," I replied simply.

For some reason this amused me. A guard at a brothel, isn't this what my mother always dreamed of… A wonderful job. Wonderfful… with two "f"s.

"Good, good," Lev Borisych immediatley interrupted me. "We're probably going to need to expand the staff. I just don't want you to leave the bar – you're experienced. We'll hire a person… Do you know anyone? You don't know anyone? We'll hire someone. One person. Think about it."

And Lev Borisych walked away. I lit a cigarette – I wasn't going to follow at his heels. I ran my boot through the water in a puddle. A car honked its horn, and I looked up: a jeep was coming around the corner, with its low beams on, a very powerful jeep, with Moscow plates. The driver, looking at me disdainfully from behind the windshield, made a harsh gesture: he raised his hands, palms up. *What are you standing there for, slowpoke!* is what this gesture means. The jeep was rolling along in neutral, but I didn't move out of the way. I would have had to move too quickly to let it past: I'm not supposed to move in a hurry, I'm not a waiter.

The driver slammed on the breaks when the jeep had almost hit me – all of this didn't take more than two seconds. I took two steps out of the way, stepping in the mud on the roadside. The jeep drove past. The driver didn't look at me.

I saw two men getting out of the jeep – one was quite short, but moved energetically, waving his arms, and kept turning his little head on a powerful neck in different directions. Even by the back of his head, I thought I could see that he smiled a lot.

There's a lot of cars today, I noticed, walking towards the club.

Molotok was looking at me with curiosity.

"Well, what was it about?" he asked in a cheerful whisper.

"They want to open a den of whores here," I replied, instantly ignoring my promises to Lev Borisych.

"And so?" Molotok asked.

"They want boys to work there as well as girls. Boys are in demand at the moment. He asked about you. He was embarrassed to ask you directly. How about it then? Want to earn some money?"

"Fuck you!" Molotok chuckled, and I also laughed.

"They need security," I said seriously, but without wiping the smile off my face.

"Why not?" Molotok said cheerfully. "What difference does it make! Will we get a raise?"

"Yes, we will," I said confidently, and then remembered that Lev Borisych hadn't said anything about the pay, not even a hint.

"Where's the turnstile here?" a new customer asked, slightly tipsy, with a moustache and smiling, but with an unpleasant strange look in his eyes. He was probably around forty.

"What turnstile?" Molotok asked.

"To put the ticket in," the man replied, smiling crookedly.

Molotok took the ticket from him with an unfriendly expression, crumpled it and threw it in the trash. The man froze there with the smile still on his unshaven face.

"Go in, go in, what are you waiting for," Molotok said hospitably.

Good on you, Syomka, I thought cheerfully, but from the expression on the man's face as he walked into the club, I realized that this was not the end: he would come back when he had thought up a reply for us.

I smoked a couple of cigarettes, traded a few jokes with Molotok, and together we appraised tonight's strippers – they arrived in a car and walked past us quickly – they always walk past quickly, never saying hello, they're unfriendly. Each one of them had a large bag over her shoulder. I always wonder what they have in their bags, if they appear on stage in a tiny top and skirt which would fit in my pocket. Maybe shoes – and that's it...

The strippers were flat-chested, and up close they were not attractive at all – with the rare type of ugliness that women can detect themselves. You often see that kind of face among prostitutes in the provinces.

At midnight, at the height of stupid, drunk merriment, with plenty of smoke breaks, the local gangsters turned up – they like to drive from club to club until morning, four young guys the same age as Molotok and me, and Diesel – one of the city "authorities", friendly, battered-looking and grey-haired. When he said hello to us, he called me by name: *Hi, Zakhar, how are you?*– and every time I noted to myself that I found it pleasant, damn me, that he remembered me, that he shook my hand and smiled.

Why the hell shouldn't I find that pleasant? I snarled to myself.

What are you so happy about? I replied to myself. *Why did you wag your tail, you mutt? You think he'll be there for you when you need help? He'll step over you without noticing, he's a wolf, wolf spawn, with the evil blood of a wolf...*

Diesel entered the room with dignity, glanced sideways at the table of "serious people" that was visible through the open screen, and immediately turned away, as if he didn't care.

Oh, Diesel, I thought poetically. *What a strong man you are, how experienced you are, people are afraid of you and respect you – but next to these men you're just a crook... Your time is coming to an end, Diesel.*

At one o'clock in the morning., winking to Molotok, I went to see the first striptease number. There were usually two numbers during the night, and Molotok and I watched them in turn – I watched the first one, he watched the second. Or we just said to hell with it all, and both went into the hall, only glancing at the entrance from time to time, to make sure no one was barging in without a ticket.

The girls were still dancing on their skinny white legs, when there was a crash in the hall. I rushed in a few seconds later, but couldn't work out what was going on: a large Caucasian, just under two meters tall, was standing alone in the middle of the hall, in a jacket for some reason. It was immediately obvious that he was one of the people responsible for the noise – but who was with him, or rather, who was against him?

I saw that the crooks and Diesel were sitting at a table in the corner, and had turned away, as if it was nothing to do with them. *And the poser is sitting with them,* I noticed out of the corner of my eye.

The crooks' heads were tense, and also a few customers sitting near them were looking sideways in their direction.

It's them, of course, I realized, but didn't do anything.

"We'll meet again!" the Caucasian said loudly, in no particular direction, as if to everyone at once; and the meaning of his words essentially came to down to an overdue attempt not to lose his dignity. "We'll come around tomorrow and talk!" he promised with an accent.

I went up to him, took him by the elbow and pulled him towards the exit:

"Come on, you can talk outside..."

For appearance's sake, he held his arm back a little, but I know gestures like this and easily tell if the person intends to resist stupidly, or if these intention can be nipped in the bud.

"Come on, come on," I pushed him in the shoulder.

"But why me?" the Caucasian said indignantly, but without much confidence; two girls followed him, both of them non-Russians, both frightened.

"Go on, go on..." I said, hearing in my voice the same unfeigned tiredness, which I know sometimes has a better effect on people than stupid shouting.

As we left the hall, the Caucasian immediately fell silent, and evidently was satisfied himself that everything had ended like this, without any bloodshed.

"What happened?" I asked Vadik, after I escorted the Caucasian out and returned to the bar. Vadik is usually aware of what goes on, he sees everything from behind his bar.

"Those guys, with Diesel... one of his guys kicked the chair out from under the Caucasian, when he went past. The Caucasian leapt to his feet..."

Well and good… I thought about the incident. … *well and good.*

As I walked away from the bar, I ran right into one of Diesel's companions, and it seemed to me that he snorted triumphantly.

What a scum… I thought, shuddering. The guy had the eyes of a maniac, white and stupid, chapped cheekbones with blond stubble, bad teeth and a narrow forehead.

I didn't feel like watching the striptease any more.

Molotok and I went outside – I had a smoke, and he got some fresh air.

Two sweaty guys jumped out of the club, one of them with his shirt unbuttoned down to his belly button, and the other all red and oily, as if he had come out of a frying pan. They were obviously going to have a fight. Their conversation, as is usual in such cases, was completely meaningless.

"So, what do you want?"

"I don't give a damn, you understand me?"

"You'll answer for it, I swear."

"Don't swear…"

"What do you want, huh?"

Molotok and I went up to them and stood there. They kept repeating their oaths, twisting their drunken, red-lipped mouths, and clenching their fists.

"You wanna fight?" I asked "Go behind the bushes and fight then, don't hang around here."

They kept standing opposite each other, pretending not to notice me.

"What did I just say?" I asked, two notes higher.

The one in the unbuttoned shirt didn't have enough strength of character to maintain the pose, and with a disgusted expression he ducked back into the club. The second turned his back to us, and lit a cigarette, loudly exhaling the smoke. The smoke swam in the light of the street lamp, slowly. Rain was falling, barely noticeable.

The worst time at the club is after one in the morning. The guys start dividing up the girls, accidentally hitting each others' shoulders, and sorting out other stupid things like that. This goes on until four in the morning. In the last hour, they are all tired and leave slowly, without saying goodbye to us, not even seeing us, looking at the floor, while others sway and can hardly move their dull eyes. At quarter to five there's hardly anyone left in the club – two or three people, who are very sluggish. Usually, I'd noticed, they didn't have any money for a taxi, and they slowly and submissively went out into the night, when we made them leave.

Laughing, we returned to the counter. Molotok stretched, cracking his strong bones. The jacket on his back tightened when he stretched out his arms.

A girl ran past us outside, and I didn't get a chance to see her face. From the back, she seemed familiar.

"Is that Vadik's girlfriend?" I asked Molotok.

Molotok nodded.

"When did she come here? I didn't see her."

"You were out walking with Lev Borisych..."

"What's with her?"

Molotok shrugged his shoulders.

The girl was evidently agitated about something. She was running toward a taxi – the drivers always park some distance away, we don't let them park by the club, so they don't stop customers from leaving their cars there.

"She forget her purse," Molotok guessed, when the girl swiftly ran back to the club.

She probably had a fight with Vadik, I barely had time to think, when suddenly Vadik himself, his face covered in pink blotches, ran into the foyer and stopped, waiting for his girlfriend.

"Where's my purse?" she asked in a subdued voice, walking in.

"With him," he replied.

"And what?"

Vadik looked at her constantly, as if he was trying to read the answer to the question on her face.

The answer came of its own accord, opening the door to the foyer with its shoulder – it was the pale guy with the bad teeth. A woman's purse was dangling from his hand.

"Why did you run away?" he asked the girl, ignoring everyone else in the foyer.

She turned away, looking through the glass at the cars, waiting for Vadik to solve the problem somehow.

Vadik was silent, looking around with a gaze that wandered without focusing on anything: he didn't see the guy with the purse, us or his girlfriend.

I didn't want to get involved, but I said:

"Give her the bag."

"Let's go in to the club, you," said the pale guy, walking past Vadik and not answering me, and dragging the girl by the elbow. "What are you acting up for, fuck it..."

"I'm talking to you, pal," I challenged him. "Give her the purse."

"I'm not your pal," he replied, without turning around. His voice was unpleasantly calm. A person who replies with this voice may turn around and aim a short and nasty punch at the face of the person who asked the question.

"You're no one to me," I replied. "Give her the bag – and go and hang out with your friends."

"We've got our own things to sort out, who's asking you to butt in?" The guy finally turned to me, and he looked completely unfriendly. "I've known this girl... for a long time. And I'm with her now," he said slowly, almost painfully, uttering the words as if he had difficulty talking. "Who are you? The vice squad? Didn't anyone explain your duties to you?"

"My duties are no concern of yours," I replied. "The bag isn't yours, even if you shared a potty with the girl at kindergarten. Give her the purse, and off you go."

The guy was silent, smiling . After a pause, showing that he wasn't obeying me, but was making an independent decision, he replied:

"I'll give it to her, but don't you stick your nose in again."

The guy gave the girl the purse, and she grabbed it, but instead of going outside she went into the club again.

"And you can go away and hide behind your bar," the guy said to Vadik, and followed the girl back into the club.

"What a brainless girl!" I said angrily, when I was alone with Syoma. "Why the hell did she go back there?"

Molotok also swore – in the sense that the pale guy was a real jerk.

She'll put a strain on his nerves all night... I thought about Vadik's girlfriend.

I felt like smoking, but unable to resist, I went to see what would happen with them next.

I didn't see the guy or Vadik's girlfriend. Vadik himself was mixing a cocktail for someone.

"Where's your girlfriend?" I said angrily over someone's shoulder: you couldn't get to the bar, it was so crowded.

"She went upstairs, to the changing room," Vadik replied, not looking me in the eye.

Why did she go there? I wondered. *No one who doesn't work here is supposed to go there.*

I had never been there myself. I went up the staircase, looking around. There seemed to be just two rooms there: for the DJ and for the dancers.

I looked into the first one – a stripper was standing in the middle of the room, topless, and adjusting her stocking. For some reason seeing her breasts didn't affect me at all – they were just breasts, I wouldn't have been any more surprised if I had seen her elbow or knee.

"Did you see a girl here?" I asked, looking at her.

"Svetka? She ran out through the other entrance. That jerk was chasing her. He came in here, he knocked."

"How do you know she's called Svetka?"

"Svetka? We studied together. She came to watch me dance tonight. You should do something, you really should, he's completely nuts. He was shouting..."

Without replying, I closed the door.

I went down the other staircase, didn't see anyone, and returned to the foyer.

"Did you see them?" I asked Syoma.

He hadn't. But they came back themselves: the girl, Svetka, now completely hysterical, with disheveled hair, and the guy behind her, with his angrily tight cheeks trembling angrily, insolent, stupid and stubborn.

"Come with me, and today I'll fuck you..." he pulled her by the shoulder, catching her by the door outside.

"You're getting on my nerves," I said.

"Who's getting on your nerves?" the guy looked at me, baring his teeth.

"You are."

I jumped off the stool, and Diesel came out – loud in every movement he made, slightly drunk, smiling – perhaps he had already found something out, perhaps from our appearance he realized that there would be a fight, but he reacted immediately.

"What are you doing here?" without malice, but loudly, with a father's honor, he questioned his pale colleague. He turned him around, and with a heavy blow with two hands on the shoulders, he thrust him out of the foyer, outside.

"Sorry, guys, he's acting the fool... Keep working, don't worry," Diesel said to us, smiling.

They left immediately.

Svetka came back to the club again, stayed there for a minute, and then Vadik came out to see her off with a tender expression.

I shook my head, thinking about Vadik, and Svetka, and about that... nasty...

"Next time we should knock him out straight away," I said to Syoma.

Syoma nodded. He agreed.

I was a bit nervous, why hide it.

But Syoma wasn't. Or he had already calmed down.

"Zakhar, I don't understand, where do they get these cars from?" he asked me for the umpteenth time.

A foreign car drove up, and inside were two guys who were virtually teenagers, but overflowing with their own expensive worth. Of course they opened the doors, and turned the stereo up loud enough to drown out the din of music in the club. They called over some girls they knew, who happened to be nearby – and the girls quietly went over to them, transfixed by the sight of the car. The teenagers smoked and laughed, nodding their heads, revealing their white necks, which Syoma could have broken with two fingers, and smoked again, and laughed – without actually getting out of the car, reclining on the luxury seats, alternately stretching their skinny legs out of the car, or tossing them up practically on the steering wheel.

"Shall we take a closer look?" Syoma called me. "It's a great car."

We went outside. Molotok went up to the car and stood next to it with a look as if he were thinking: shall I take it off them, or shouldn't I bother just yet.

Syoma had a reverent attitude towards cars. He had a beautiful, slender, large-breasted wife, whom he sometimes beat a little, because she didn't want to cook. His wife would take offense and go and stay with her mother, but then come back, because essentially he was a good guy and loved her very much.

But as I said, all he dreamt about was a car.

I stood on the steps outside the club, breathing in the fine night air and calming, calming myself down.

I couldn't care less about them, I thought, with a clear heart, which was now beating evenly. *All I need to do is finish the day's work, and that's it. And tomorrow will be a new day, but that's just tomorrow... Who cares, that's right. I don't care at all about them...*

At home I have a young son and a tender wife. They're asleep now. My wife is keeping my empty place in our bed, and sometimes she strokes her hand over the space where I should be lying.

Our son wakes up two or three times a night and asks for kefir. He isn't quite yet two years old. My wife gives him a bottle, and he falls asleep, smacking his lips.

My son always looks as if he were sitting on a riverbank, swinging his leg, and looking at the swift water.

He has flaxen hair which gives out a soft light. For that reason, I call him "Birch bud." The name suits him very well.

Smiling at my thoughts, I went down to where Syoma was standing.

He certainly liked the car. But not the guys in the car.

He seemed to be chewing on a crooked smile, as he walked around the car. The girls were already staring at Syoma, and the guys started spitting a lot, in long streams.

"Piggies, right?" Syoma finally said loudly, he was standing on the other side of the car, by the trunk.

I raised my eyes in surprise.

"The piggies took money from papa and mama and are showing off," Syoma explained.

I started choking with laughter.

Molotok walked past the driver, who was smoking, with his legs crossed, and the girls who had suddenly stopped talking, and shrank back in fear at the sight of the sullen security guard.

Suddenly Molotok stopped, and went back to the open car door.

"Right?" he said loudly to the guy behind the wheel, as if speaking to a deaf person. Molotok even inclined his powerful head, as if he seriously wanted to hear a reply.

"What?" the guy asked, instinctively drawing his head away.

"Nothing," Molotok replied in a go-to-hell tone of voice, and pushed the car door. It hit the guy's legs, but not hard.

Out of the club, opening his mouth either to the wind or the absent rain, came the guy who had asked us where the turnpike was.

"We didn't go around like that in Afghanistan..." he said with drunk irony, looking over Molotok and me as we returned to the foyer.

He's in the mood now, just as I thought...

"What did he say, I didn't understand?" Molotok asked, when we sat on our stools.

I shrugged my shoulders. I didn't understand either. He himself didn't even understand what he had said. But he needed to open his mouth, sluiced with vodka, so he did.

He was clearly dying to say something else: in a hurry, taking several drags in a row, he smoked half a cigarette and returned to us, after some confusion as to what side the door opened on. He entered the foyer, and stood there, swaying and smiling. He didn't shut his mouth, and you could see his nicotine-stained but still strong teeth. For some reason he undid the bag from around his waist, and held it in his hand.

People coming in off the street avoided him.

"What are you standing in the middle of the road for, like a weed?" I asked with interest.

"Am I in the way?" he asked maliciously.

I didn't reply.

He came over to our table and put the bag on it.

He fumbled for a long time in the pockets, looking for something, cigarettes evidently.

He put some papers out on the counter, and small change.

He finally found the packet with broken cigarettes in it, covered in tobacco.

"Keep an eye on my bag," he said, squinting with a drunken, mocking look. "I'll have another smoke."

"Take it away," I asked him simply.

"Go on," he said, and turned to the exit.

I lightly hit the bag, and it flew into the corner of the foyer, by the garbage bin.

"So that's how you are," he drawled, turning around. "In Afghanistan…"

"…A mushroom looks like a man. I told you: take it away."

He stood there for a while, rocking on his heels again. Then he picked up the bag from the floor. He looked it over for another minute.

He came up to me, and unexpectedly threw his right arm around my neck, either to embrace or strangle me.

"So that's how you are…how you are…" he muttered, hoarsely and maliciously.

Molotok looked at me, swearing, but by my face he realized that everything was all right.

Without hurrying too much, with my right hand I found the thumb of the sinewy, strong hand encircling me and pulled it hard, jabbing the man in the chest with my left elbow at the same time.

Grunting, the man let me go. I grabbed him by the chest.

"What's with you, Afghan jerk? Don't wanna dance? Huh? Why don't you dance, soldier? You bored or something?" I shook him. "Get out of here then!"

I pushed him out on to the street, almost roaring with irritation. I couldn't control myself, and rushed after him, and pushed him off the stone steps of the club.

Syoma also came outside. He looked at me, smiling tenderly.

"Angry?" he asked me, looking at the "Afghan," who had started searching for cigarettes again, not far away. "Angry, Zakhar?" Syoma asked me again, but in such a way that I didn't have to answer, and it wouldn't offend him. And I didn't answer. Just because I was immediately distracted.

Something nasty was happening in the car park.

The Moscow guys who I had met outside had parked their massive jeep so that it blocked a smaller jeep. But in the smaller jeep, the five "serious people", as Molotok and I called them, were sitting.

For three minutes now, their jeep had been blocked. This is a long time for "serious people" – three minutes. To start with, they honked their horn – when I was talking with the "Afghan" I heard the horn – but no one came out to them.

Now, two of the "serious people" had climbed out of their car, and one of them, with a certain zest, was kicking the wheel of the Moscow guests' jeep. The alarm went off, it blared for 10 seconds, then stopped, and he kicked the wheel again, getting angrier each time.

I should probably go and call to those… Moscow bastards… I thought, but I didn't go anywhere, and decided to stand and smoke, and watch: it was impossible to tear myself away from the sight of these furious, very strong men.

"Now something's going to happen," Molotok said cheerfully. Even he got this feeling, though usually his intuition is napping.

I nodded my head slightly, as if in time with the music: going to happen, going to happen, going to happen.

The Muscovites turned up, languid, smiling, when I was already looking the cigarette butt over, working out where to throw it: to walk over to the garbage can or let it lie here, under my feet.

Of the Moscow guests, only the driver looked annoyed – it was his car, after all, that was being kicked. But from all appearances it was clear that the driver was not in charge. Two of his passengers initially didn't even go down the stairs of the club to the car, but talked about something, looking around, laughing.

The taller one squinted, looking at the back of the driver walking towards the jeep. The second, who seemed to be just one and a half meters tall, cheerfully shook his head and rubbed his small hands together. For some reason, it seemed that his palms were rough.

The driver approached the car with deliberate slowness. The "serious people" were waiting for him, not moving. Their faces were calm, as usual.

At the door of his jeep, the driver stopped, in no hurry to open it. I didn't notice who spoke first, he or the people waiting for him, and I also didn't hear what they said – the music blaring in the club drowned it out.

The tall Muscovite seemed to want to go to the car, but his companion with the rough palms held him back by the sleeve. There was something devious about the short man's behavior – he was clearly not afraid of anything, and even… on the contrary… he was waiting for it, yes.

The poser came out of the club, but went back in immediately, sensing something.

Something seemed to have happened by the jeep, they just pushed the driver lightly in the shoulder, and he also swung his arm, but that's hardly a fight, or a cause for one. There was no fight or cause for it, nothing – but swiftly, the short guy, as if he were on all fours, leapt off the steps, and I lost sight of him, only guessing what had happened a few seconds later, when two of the "serious people" standing by the jeep suddenly disappeared from view. They fell down.

Not believing my eyes, I moved towards the jeep. At the same time, another three "serious people" jumped out of their car.

While Molotok and I approached, these three also fell into puddles. But the two who were the first to fall got up – but didn't remain standing long either.

There wasn't any fight. No one swung their arms or jumped, and there was no nasty sound of people being punched in the face.

The short guy, as if amusing himself, moved from one opponent to the next, knocking them down with an imperceptible movement, and they, all of them as large as bears, all of them already dirty, with sweaters torn at the collars, fell over immediately, not even managing to swing their arms, or whatever else you can swing when you really want to hit someone.

Out of inertia, I plunged right into the thick of the fighters – or rather, the people who were trying to fight – and ended up just two meters away from the short guy. He turned to me. He still had the same smile on his face, and it seemed that he winked as he moved towards me with dancing, gentle movements.

I realized that in a second or so I would also be lying on the asphalt.

"Take it easy there!" I said cheerfully, looking him in the eyes, only his eyes, as I moved back, stretching out my arms in front of me with my palms open, and still hoping to hit him at least once, or better, more than once, if he made a movement, any movement towards me, against me.

"I'll kick him… I'll kick him in the shin, in the bone," I decided, smiling happily. For a few seconds, like brothers, we looked at each other, with love.

Here he was distracted, as one of the "serious people," who was rolling in the mud in a very non-serious way, jumped up from the side, and immediately fell over, but the short guy was already moving off, cheerful and lively.

His companion, I noticed, wasn't fighting at all, but was shouting very fiercely, running up to the people who had been knocked over, and grabbing some of them by the hair.

"What's wrong, assholes? Don't feel well? Bet it's a long time since you got a fright like this," he said.

By the time that the man who had been knocked over had stood up, the Muscovite was standing by another who was rolling in the puddle. It seemed that he found it more convenient to talk to a person who was lying down. Their driver got into the car and was warming the engine, even smoking while he did so.

He's the one I should talk to, I realized.

"Don't get involved!" I shouted to Molotok, and I ran around to the driver of the Moscow jeep.

"Get your car out of here!" I shouted at his face. "Get it out of here, I said!"

He reacted to my voice, put the car in reverse and then stopped, unable to see anything in the rear vision mirror.

"Molotok, if there's anyone under the wheels, drag them out of the way!" I shouted.

Syoma nodded, dragged someone out by the legs, and waved at me to let the car drive away.

The jeep, reflecting light off its powerful body, drove off, and I followed its movement with my eyes. I happened to notice that the two teenagers in the foreign car whom Molotok had harassed were standing not far from the club.

They're waiting for us to get beaten up, the jerks... They want to come and finish us off, the vultures...

The "serious people" had already worked out what to do without my help – at least, one of them had. He got behind the wheel and also tried to drive away – to get out of there while the road was clear.

"Molotok, put them in the car!" I shouted.

Waiting for the jeep belonging to the "serious people" to drive out of the car park and on to the exit road that was lit by streetlamps, I opened three of the doors, except the driver's door, and started to gather up the guys who had been beaten up.

"Go on, get out of here!" I either asked or ordered, lifting up the heavy but limp men, and dragged them over to the car, pushing them inside.

Another two were left. The cheerful, dwarf-like guy was patiently waiting for them to get up so that he could knock them over again, and was not letting anyone near his victims.

"Calm your friend down, let them go," I addressed the tall Muscovite, who was red and agitated.

"They should be crushed, those animals!" he shouted. "Who do they think they're dealing with! Crushed!"

"Come on, get him out of there, I've had enough!" I shouted, and pushed him unexpectedly roughly, and this had an effect on him.

Throwing out his arms as if to embrace him, the tall man blocked his short friend for a few moments, and this was enough time for Molotok and me. We pushed the remaining two into the car. One of the men had blood running down his face, from somewhere under his hair. The jeep belonging to the "serious people" drove off.

The armored black beast from Moscow once more drove back towards the club building, slowly parked and fell silent.

"Go get them! Crush them!" the tall Muscovite shouted again stupidly, but the short guy waved his hand and went back into the club, almost jumping up the steps.

Lev Borisych appeared – first his head poked out from behind the door and looked around swiftly, and then the rest of him.

"What happened? Did something happen?" he asked quietly, casting his eyes all around, as if to see if something valuable had fallen to the ground somewhere nearby.

"Everything's fine, Lev Borisych," I replied, smiling. "People got a little bit carried away... Everything's fine."

"Nothing got broken? No one got hurt?"

"Nothing's broken, everyone's fine, Lev Borysych."

And he left, looking around, but without finding anything.

"Zakhar, good on you!" Syoma acknowledged cheerfully. "Ah? That damn samurai would have wasted us. How did you guess that they had to be driven away?"

"I looked into his eyes, and realized it immediately," I replied, also smiling.

For three minutes or so, we couldn't stop laughing, re-telling each other how it all happened.

It's a good feeling when you think that the worst is over. There wasn't much time left now: soon it would be morning.

A girl wearing a dress that suited her wonderfully came out to us in the foyer, smiling. She had a large, pure face, definitely beautiful. She had high heels, calm hands and manners. The only thing is that she was not so young, around thirty-three. But can you call that a shortcoming?

"What happened here?" she asked, only looking at me.

To be honest, I had noticed her when she arrived at the club – alone. And then, when she was sitting on a tall stool, sipping a cocktail at the bar also alone, I saw her again. I thought: *She's very beautiful, and so no one goes straight up to her. They don't believe that she came here by herself.... And as if those kids are going to go up to her, the jerks...*

Molotok immediately grasped the situation – he has no instinct for anything, but at these moments he does.

"I'll go and look how things are going inside..." he said quietly and left. I didn't need him to do that, but Molotok wouldn't believe me.

"There was a fight, a bunch of idiots..." I replied, calmly looking at the smiling face.

I'm no psychologist, and not a collector of thin hands open to be read, or hot and compliant bodies – but I guessed everything from the way that she looked at me.

She looked at me without taking her eyes away – right in the eyes, with a clear smile on her occasionally trembling lips.

"Why do you always wear a beret?" she asked.

Just as I thought, she didn't care about the fight, who was fighting whom. She had to ask me something, and so she did – and forgot about her questions straight away.

"A beret?" I asked and got a cigarette – not because I was anxious, but just because I hadn't smoked for a while.

While I was taking it out of the packet, I thought that she had to notice the wedding ring on my ring finger.

But she was indifferent to the ring, and kept smiling, looking me over, sometimes slightly tilting her head to the side.

Grown-up women like this can hold pauses, listen to pauses, and not hurry at all. You don't have to keep a conversation going with them, you can look at each other, as if playing a simple game: *well, what are you like? You're beautiful, right? And looking at me? Why?*

And she answers all these questions without saying anything.

Her answers were also in the form of questions: *don't you understand yourself?* – this is how she replied silently – *you've understood already, haven't you?*

Yes, I had.

"I wear a beret because I don't have hair on my head, and if I sit like this all evening, without a beret, the customers find it very interesting, and sometimes amusing."

I took off my beret, revealing my shaven head. This was a very open gesture, almost intimate: *look, you asked me to.* If she had taken off her shoe and placed her foot on my knee: *… look at how I've painted my toenails…* it would have been almost the same thing.

She stretched out her hand – to stroke my head, to see if it was prickly – but I caught her by the wrist with a light, almost cat-like movement.

"You're so… nimble. Do you really object?"

You talk so well, I thought. *Many girls have talked to me here, but none of them asked me like this: …do you really object…*

"Please don't," I said, and having held it less than an instant, I let go her hand, which pulsed in my fingers, with thin veins, warm and tender, like a bird.

If I had held it, then the melody which it seemed that we had already begun to play, listening to each other, would have continued. But I didn't.

She didn't believe it right away: she probably didn't want to believe that everything had been cut off so quickly. She thought that I was a little embarrassed.

She smiled, recovering, but the smile hung in the air, as no one responded to it.

I took a long drag, and slowly breathed out the smoke. Finally, I also smiled, but with a different smile, in a different register: *nothing's going to happen, no melody, I'm not playing*. And I put my beret on.

"Well, I'll go and dance some more," she said cheerfully.

"When you dance, I'll come and watch you," I replied in the same tone.

She went away, and I knew that she would never come back to me again. And I didn't regret it. I looked at the filter of the cigarette. It was just the sixth that night. What a horrible night, it was protecting my health. Sometimes I manage to smoke a whole packet. And this was just the sixth, which I threw away, missing the bin.

I looked at the clock: it was a little after three.

No, had I really smoked so little... I took out the packet. There were only six cigarettes missing, indeed.

My head was aching. I wanted to go home, I was sick of everyone.

The waitress came running over, she was new, Alya was her name. I didn't know what sort of name this was, Alya. Perhaps it was short for Alina.

"Listen, go and tell that prick not to touch me. He keeps touching my leg," Alya said, flaring her nostrils.

"What prick?"

"Come on, I'll show you."

Why does she think it's my job to drive men away from her, I thought lazily, sliding off the stool. *She's put on the shortest skirt you can imagine. And she shows her legs... they're beautiful... to everyone. 'Come on, I'll show you' – that's a way to talk... after all, I don't tell her where to go.*

She has long legs, yes, only she herself isn't attractive. But her legs are wonderful.

"That guy."

I nodded and went up to the table where the three Moscow guests were sitting. It was their driver who had been stroking the waitress's leg. He watched me coming over.

"Please, don't touch the waitresses anymore," I said, leaning over. "OK?"

The driver shrugged his shoulders.

"I didn't touch anyone."

"All the better," I replied and walked away.

Silly sheep, I thought again. *She should wear a more decent skirt, she's not at a children's matinee performance…*

I had only just got back to the foyer – it was empty, which was not allowed, because someone could get in without a ticket – I had just walked in, when the tall Muscovite stopped me, touching me on the shoulder.

"You insulted my friend," he said.

"I didn't insult anyone," I replied, tired. But this was a different, almost weak-willed tiredness, not the one I felt at the start of the evening, that arose from predictable human insolence, which I could break so easily.

"He didn't touch anyone, and you insulted him, you ruined his evening."

"What do you mean, he didn't touch anyone, if she's complaining?" I said. Molotok was still away somewhere.

"He didn't touch her," his voice was well-modulated, and as he talked he trembled with an approaching fury that was prepared to break out, which I had nothing to resist with. "I think you should go and apologize," he said.

To hell with it all, I thought and went back to the table.

"Your friend says that you didn't touch anyone," I said to the driver, who was looking away. "If that's so, then I apologize. I hope everything was as you say. In any case, our girls should be left alone when they're working."

The short guy, the one whom Syoma called a "samurai," was drinking juice through a straw, and his face grimaced, like a little monkey about to sneeze.

I still went back into the foyer, and even went outside, feeling as if I had suddenly lost a lot of blood.

Thirty meters or so from the club, the foreign car still had all its lights on, and the teenagers whom Molotok had insulted were sitting in the car.

Vadik came out, seeming embarrassed.

"Zakhar… That tall Muscovite… He told Alya that they'd kill her if she complained."

I nodded, unable to decide what to do.

I held a cigarette in my hands, and for the first time I didn't feel like smoking, I felt a little sick, and my head was spinning. I went into the hall, and the first thing I saw was the poser. His drunken and sweaty face was blurred, as if he had no face muscles.

Molotok appeared from somewhere.

"Everything OK?" he asked.

I nodded again: all OK.

"Where were you?" I asked, although I didn't care.

"That 'Afghan' is in the club again," Molotok said, not hearing the question. "He ran in while we were getting rid of those jerks… Shall I throw him out?"

"No, don't," I replied.

The poser walked past us, brushing me with his shoulder.

"Something has to be done," I thought. "Something has to be done. I need to pull myself together. They're like animals, they feel everything…"

"He's got a glass," Molotok nodded towards the poser.

"Sir, you can't take glasses outside," I said to the poser.

He stared at me disdainfully, took a sip of wine and spat it out on the steps, almost hitting the girl who was standing below.

"Go back inside," I asked again.

"Weren't you already told how to behave?" the poser replied, turning his blurry, disgusting face to me; in his thick-lipped open mouth, like something alive, ready to fall out, his moist, thick tongue moved.

God, how does he know, I thought miserably.

"Behave like you were told," the poser said.

I swallowed thick saliva and saw that the "Afghan" was standing nearby, making strange movements with his fingers, as if he was flexing them, and was listening to us.

The rain began to fall again, slowly and sparsely.

The tall Muscovite walked past us, haughtily, with a very satisfied expression on his face, and was already walking down the steps, when he suddenly turned around.

"So, you got it, right?" he said to me loudly.

I didn't reply. Molotok looked around uncomprehendingly, looking me in the face a couple of times.

"Didn't you hear me?" the Muscovite asked, turning back and walking right up to me.

"I can hear everything," I said distinctly.

He nodded and went to the jeep.

The "Afghan" behind my back laughed hoarsely. The poser made strange movements with his face, as if he wasn't letting something inside his mouth jump out.

"You were told, you can't take glasses out with you," Molotok, who had no idea what was going on, finally said to the poser.

"Don't touch me," the poser replied, and turned back, accidentally splashing wine on Molotok's chest, and returned to the club.

"Shit!" Molotok cursed in a whisper and began to brush the wine off his chest.

"You got wet, guys!" the "Afghan" shouted and laughed again.

"Fuck off," Molotok said to him, and the "Afghan" found this even more funny, he was already hoarse with laughter.

We returned to our counter and sat down on the stools. I leant my head against the wall, pushing the beret to the back of my head and revealing my wet forehead.

"What's wrong?" Molotok asked. "I don't get it. What happened?"

"Nothing," I replied. "You can see for yourself that nothing happened."

"Why did that tall guy talk to you like that then?"

Molotok fell silent, dissatisfied. He didn't like my replies. He thought to himself, and you could see how hard it was for him to think without expressing his thoughts out loud.

The club patrons began to disperse.

I sat at the counter, trying not to see anyone or think about anything, but for some reason I imagined that everyone walking past was looking ironically at me. It seemed intolerable – but I endured it, I put up with it, and smoked...

The packet was running out. I didn't take it off the counter anymore.

The girl who had come up to me – *...imagine, I didn't ask her name...* I thought – also walked past me without saying a word, without even nodding her head. She took a taxi and drove away in it without turning around. I looked at her from behind the glass, for some reason waiting for her to turn around. It was important.

Molotok kept silent, sometimes watching me taking out a new cigarette, then turning around immediately as soon as I lit up – so he didn't have to look me in the face.

The "Afghan" stood on the steps for a little longer, still swaying, and sometimes twisting his face into a smile. Then he waved a hand in our direction, and, swaying, walked away.

At about five in the morning, once he had calculated the takings, Lev Borisych rolled past, and left without saying goodbye. He never said goodbye, in fact.

Disdainfully clicking her heels, Alya went out to smoke. Twisting up her unattractive face, taking a deep drag, she stood to us half-turned, so I could see her and understand what she thought of me. Vadik came out after her, cheerful for some reason.

He also lit up, to keep Alya company. He smokes one cigarette a night – right at this time, at five in the morning, when the sun is coming up.

What a sour sunrise it was today. It was swill, not a sunrise.

The Muscovites were almost the last to leave. Devoid of emotions, with an empty head, I waited for the tall guy to stop again and say something to me, but hiccupping loudly, he was talking with the driver, and walked past me as if I no longer existed.

The poser followed him, and stopped in the foyer to put on his coat. I watched him waving it around, bathing us in the stench of barely perceptible rot. The poser was in a hurry, and wanted to say something to the Moscow guests, but he was too late, and they drove off, stepping on the gas and brazenly honking at everyone who was wandering in the road.

The poser went outside. When Vadik saw him, he dived back into the club, but got a chubby hand on his backside. The poser grinned happily at Vadik's vanishing back, and when he saw us he loudly gathered a mouthful of saliva and spat, hitting the glass door. The thick yellow spit, like a crushed and chewed mollusk, ran down the glass.

I jumped off the stool, and it fell down, crashing behind me.

The poser hurried down the steps.

He hailed a taxi, waving his arm. *...He doesn't want to drive his own car, he's drunk...* I realized. The taxi drove towards him – but I got to him first.

Turning the poser around by his shoulder, I did something that I never allowed myself to do to the club patrons – I punched him in the face, in the jaw, with a good, solid blow. I caught him by the coat, not letting him fall. I grabbed him by the hair, which was oily and slippery, straightened his head up and punched him again, aiming for his teeth.

I let the poser go, and he fell down face forwards, dripping blood, spit and something else.

"He's not going anywhere," I said to the taxi driver in an even voice. The taxi driver nodded and drove off.

Molotok, with a red face, kicked the poser in the ribs with his heavy boot. He jolted from the blow. Coughing, he got on all fours and tried to crawl away. I stepped on his coat.

"Don't go away," I said to him.

Molotok kicked him again – in the stomach, and I thought I saw something fall out of his mouth.

His arms weakened, he couldn't stay on all fours, and he fell face down, with his chin in the pond, blowing red bubbles which kept bursting.

I squatted down next to him, grabbed a firm hold of the hair on the back of his head, and several times, seven I think, I smashed his head, his face, his nose, his lips, against the asphalt. I wiped my hand on his coat, but it still remained dirty, slimy and disgusting.

Only then did I notice that the foreign car... with those teenagers in it... was still there. They were watching us from behind the glass.

Looking around, I found a rock. They realized what I was looking for, and they rapidly turned the car around, its brakes squealing.

"Get the fuck out of here!" I shouted, throwing the rock, but it didn't reach them.

Molotok also found a rock, but it was too late to throw it. Rocking the stone in his hand, he threw it into the grass by the roadside.

"Bye, Syoma," I said almost inaudibly.

"Yes, let's," he replied hoarsely.

At home, my wife was sitting in the kitchen.

"I'm very tired," she said, not turning around.

Taking off my boots, tearing them off, as they were stuck, I looked at the back of my wife's head.

The child in our room began to cry.

"Could you go to him?" she asked.

I went into the bathroom, and turned on a jet of cold, almost icy water. I put my hands under it.

"Could you?" she asked again.

I stubbornly rubbed my wrists, palms and fingers with soap, so that the soap got under my clipped nails. I put my hands under the water yet again and looked at what was pouring off them.

The child cried in the room alone.

There won't be anything

Two sons are growing up.

One of them is four months old. He wakes up at night; he doesn't cry, no. He lies on his stomach, supports himself on his elbows, raises his white-domed little head and breathes. In short, fast breaths, like a dog following a scent.

I don't turn the light on.

I listen to him.

"Where are you running to, lad?" I ask hoarsely in the darkness.

He breathes.

His head gets tired, and it hits the mattress of the child's bed. Oops, there's the rubber nipple under his face. He understands everything, the wise minnow – he twists his head, takes the nipple between his lips and sucks.

If he gets tired of the nipplr, there is a soft noise – it falls out. And he breathes again.

From his breathing, I guess that he has turned his head and is looking into the darkness: *I can't see anything.*

...But I want to sleep.

"Ignat, you're a rascal," I say sullenly.

He falls silent for a moment and listens: *Where do I know that voice from?*

My head is heavy like a damp burdock in autumn – nothing sticks to it, except sleep, dragging downward, into sticky mud.

Initially I turned the light on when I was woken up by his breathing – he was happy then. Every night we talked until dawn on the couch. I put my son next to me, and we talk. He grimaces, I laugh, keeping my mouth shut, so as not to scare him. Now I don't turn on the light, I'm tired.

I don't even remember the minute when he falls asleep, because I've fallen into unconsciousness earlier myself.

At night I wake up once, sometimes twice – in sinful fatherly horror: *Where is he? What's that? I can't hear him breathing!*

But if it's getting light already, the darkness is fading – I pull the cover from the bed and see him there: his face is like an onion bulb, and he's quietly snuffling.

I like to kiss him when he wakes up. With my lips I touch his cheeks, filled with the milk of my darling, and I am enraptured.

Lord, how tender he is. Like the flesh of a melon.

And his breath… What is the blooming of the shaggy flowers of spring to me – my son snuffles by my face, radiant as though after Communion.

I raise him up above me – his two cheeks hang down, and his saliva drips onto my chest.

I jiggle him to make him laugh. Do you know how they laugh? Like sheep: *Ba-a-a-a.*

I throw him up gently, without stretching my arms. He doesn't laugh. But he twists his head: *Aha, this is where I live…*

"Bleat like a sheep, Ignatka, come on"! I jiggle him. He doesn't want to. He's sick of being shaken, he's going to get grumpy.

I put the baby on my chest, and his feet kick me in the stomach. He raises himself up on his elbows, and looks at my head. He gets tired of this, and lowers his head: *A beard, viewed close up. And inter-es-ting beard. If I could just figure out how to chew it.*

I stroke his warm head. It seems to be covered in soft fat.

I'll pester the baby and look him over until my darling wakes up in the next room.

We have a large apartment, two spacious rooms with high ceilings are divided by a corridor. In the second room on the lower bunk of a two-level bed, my darling is asleep. I sent her there in the evening so that she would get some sleep. And on the upper bunk is my elder son, five years old, an angelic nature, and my eyes. His name is Gleb.

She's woken up, my flower, and seeing her reassures and soothes me. She comes towards me shyly:

"Get any sleep?"

She's not asking about me, but about him. Because if he was asleep, then I would also have had some dreams.

She kisses us in turn, but him first. She says tender words to him. She only smiles at me. Then she places her palms under her breasts – they're heavy, I can see it too.

"It's built up," she says.

"He'll drink it for you," I replied. "He won't mind."

He never cries, not even when he's hungry. He only sometimes starts to whine, without any tears, as if he's complaining: *I'm lying here by myself, guys, is it hard to amuse me? For example, I like to look at the bookshelves, when I'm carried past them. There are a lot of different colors in them.*

When he was born, he didn't cry either, I saw it myself, I was there; he didn't cry at the hospital either, and during his first days at home he lay there, entranced, and looked attentively at the world. Only on the third day of our life together, when I went into the kitchen to check on the cabbage soup, I heard a baby's offended cry.

I ran to him – and immediately guessed what was going on.

"Did you pinch him, you little bitch?" I asked my darling, hiding a smile.

"I thought he was dumb," she replied.

Although I forgot – once he did cry his eyes out.

Spoiled by his constantly good mood, my darling and I ran out to the shop, leaving the children at home. To buy sweet biscuits for mama and bitter wine for the father. When we came back, we could already hear a terrible wailing, and in two voices.

I flew up the stairs, kicking my shoes into the corridor – my younger son was bawling in his bed, already hoarse, and my elder son had shut himself in the toilet, and was screaming his head off.

"Ignatka, dear!" said the father to the younger son.

"Glebushka, darling," said the mother to the elder son.

"Mama, help Ignatka!" Gleb sobbed into my darling's stomach. "I can't make him quiet!"

He felt sorry for his brother.

Soon Gleb will appear, wandering in on his long awkward legs, my luminous child.

And we will all be together, three men and one girl.

She is very pleased that there are three of us and one of her. My darling never wanted to give birth to someone in her own image. Perhaps because she herself was an eccentric and headstrong girl herself, until I clutched my greedy hand around her wrist and gave her my child to bear – to the detriment of her girlish lightness, but to the benefit of her human wisdom.

Now the children strengthen and build our love. Gleb often says:

"Guilt should always be divided in half."

He sometimes runs to his mother – he kisses her hurriedly, and then rushes to me, and also kisses me. As if we ourselves had kissed in reconciliation – we weren't sitting in different corners of our kitchen for no reason. And what to do after this? We all three laugh together and run to Ignatka's call to prayer.

You forgot about me! he says without words, conveying his idea like this:

"Ivau! Ga!" and something else, avoiding the alphabet.

We compare how the first has grown, and how the second is growing. They are very different.

The elder liked order, he ate at specific times, slept for a certain number of hours, and woke up with an accuracy to the minute. The younger knows nothing about order, no matter how hard we've tried to teach him. He wakes up and goes to sleep when he feels like it; he may eat fifteen times a day, or ask for the breast four times over three days. He has his own inner laws, and good on him – the main thing is that he be in a good mood.

The younger brother is friends with the elder. For example, however much I jiggle him, the baby does not laugh much. But as soon as Gleb comes along, the younger brother is prepared to play and almost jumps with his stomach, as if he could make a leap like a clever frog – from the bed into the couch, and from there on to the floor. Gleb starts to turn somersaults, or knead the pillow – Ignat laughs so hard that I am afraid for him.

And most remarkably, as soon as the parents enter the room, the laughter stops: *Don't interfere! We're having our own fun here.*

Our sons haven't gone far from each other, they have an understanding as if they were from one tribe, and my darling and I were from another. Perhaps it's a similar tribe, but it's still another. But it's a friendly one, of course. And it even pays a tribute. And it's happy that it has to pay the tribute. Otherwise, what could it do with this wealth of strength, health and love of organization? Must it really be given to each other? Then it would run out quicker.

Ignat snuffles at the milky breast.

He's sucked my darling dry, the little white beast.

And he holds the breast tenderly with his hands, as if he's afraid to spill something. Sometimes he jerks: *Ah, the milk has stopped flowing!*

"What are you worried about, Ignat," my darling says to him, giving a welcoming nipple to the fussing child. He closes his eyes in bliss.

Now his brother has turned up. His face is sleepy, his arms are dangling, and a morning branch is sticking up in his underpants.

"Good morning, Gleb."

"Good morning, Papa. Good morning, Mama."

He goes up to Ignat and touches his ear.

"Shhh..." Mama says. "Don't bother him."

He likes to disturb us and get in the way, talk constantly, ask questions, answer them, philosophize, make comments, generalization and far-reaching conclusions – far beyond his judgment, experience and understanding.

He can feel a change in his parents' mood with invariable precision, a slight hint of bewilderment from his father, which would inevitably turn into anger – if not for the son.

"Papa, don't swear!"

"I'm not swearing yet, Gleb," I say in a cold voice.

"You already are..." he says very confidently.

You can't hide from his confidence, you can't get around it, to jump out of another corner, carrying your cherished resentment on your deeply unshaven face. Because while you go around it, you forget what the resentment tasted like and what color it was, and from what bacteria it appeared on earth.

My darling addresses Gleb like an oracle, like a wise man, as if he were not a rosy child on long legs, but a wise seraphim.

"Glebushka, what do you think, did I act correctly?"

Or – in a woman's shop:

"Glebushka, which gloves do you like the best – with buckles or without?"

They like him at kindergarten, and he is accepted by the boys in our yard – although they are older than him by two, three or even four years; during family excursions to the shop, Gleb is greeted by the charming young girls from the neighboring dormitory with incredible, almost playful tenderness:

"Hi Gleb! Look," the tender-faced blond girl says to her friend "It's Gleb!"

"Hi there, Gleb!" the second girl cheerfully says.

And they look at him as if they are almost in love. They don't even look at me. Damn it, they don't even look at his father.

Gleb replies to the girls calmly, taking their joy as something for granted.

"Gleb, who are they?" my darling asks, as soon as we walk away from the girls.

He tells us their names – Vika and Olesya. And that's it, no more information but that.

I once heard them talking – at the playground in the yard. I walked past the wooden fence and saw that these beauties were laughing, looking at Gleb – not patronizingly, in the way that youths make fun of children, but quite heartily. Gleb, waiting for them to stop laughing, continued his story, and furthermore in different characters.

It seems to me that his vocabulary is much larger than most of the guys who are the same age as these girls. Every time I walk by the dormitory, there are males smoking by the entrance – and I feel an urge to interrupt someone's profane mumblinb:

Doesn't it upset you that you're already twenty years old, and you're still a complete moron?

I'm probably getting old, if I've become so irritable. Ten years ago I drank a wonderfully large amount of alcoholic beverages with guys like this – and at the time I thought they were fine fellows.

I'm getting old, I didn't even go to the girls who were being entertained by Gleb at the playground. When I saw myself as a lively father perched on the neighboring bench with some stupid phrase on his lips such as *Having fun there? – when* I imagined this picture, I squirmed all over with disgust.

And I'm not even thirty.

I'm not even thirty, and I'm happy.

I don't think about the frailty of life, I haven't cried in seven years – since the moment that my darling told me that she loved me and would be my wife. Since then I haven't found any reason to cry, and I laugh a lot, and even more often I smile in the middle of the street – at my thoughts, at my darlings, who with their three hearts lightly beat the melody of my happiness.

And I stroke my darling's back, and my children's heads, and I also stroke my unshaven cheeks, and my palms are warm, outside the window there is snow and spring, snow and winter, snow and autumn. This is my Homeland, and we live in it.

Only sometimes my elder son ruins my mood with his voice, persistent as a stick:

"Mama, does everyone die, or not everyone?"

"Only the body dies, son. The soul is immortal."

"I don't like that."

I avoid these conversations and smoke in the corridor. Pointlessly, as if I am intentionally halting the movement of my thoughts, I stare at the wall.

I thought about this for the first time when I was a little older than he is now – probably when I was seven.

In my grey village, which was only slightly pink in the evenings, I hacked with my little axe at the woodchips spread out on a stump when this thought unexpectedly doused my childish heart with clammy cold – and from horror bordering on anger, I hit my finger, splitting the nail in half.

Afraid to scare my grandma, who was turning hay not far away, I hid my hand, clenched it in a fist with the index finger sticking out, dripping red and smarting terribly.

My grandma – I called her "Gramma" – immediately guessed that something unpleasant had happened, and she was already running to me, asking:

"Dearie…what is it? What's happened… dearie?"

Then only I twisted my lips, and my tears burst out – they ran and flowed down all the sides of my childish face, the reflection of which I often try to see in the faces of my children.

Grama bandaged my finger, and I didn't tell her anything, and never told anyone about it in my life, because I completely stopped thinking about it.

Death, as annoying as the toothache, I only remembered when I heard my son, and I had completely forgotten the incident with the axe – it unexpectedly appeared in my memory together with the clamminess in my heart, and the feeling of bleeding flesh, when my darling told me:

"There was a phone call. Your grandma is dead. Gramma."

The village where I grew up is a long way away. It takes a long time to get there, and trains don't go there.

I went to the garage, to my large, white car.

There was a large, white snow lying by the garage, and I spent a long time clearing it away with a spade, and was soon wet and angry.

Then I used a crowbar to crack the ice that seemed to be trying to get into the garage. The broken ice lay in crooked, sharp pieces on the snow and on the uncovered asphalt.

I spent a long time warming up the car, and I smoked, sweating, exhausted, broken into frozen pieces myself – a shard of white forehead flashed in the rear vision mirror, and a white, freezing hand holding a cigarette stuck out the window.

Ten minutes later I pulled out of the garage, hearing the crack of ice and the crunch of snow under the wheels.

It was completely dark now, and it was clear that I would have to drive all night to help my grandfather organize the funeral.

I ran home, and my darling came out to meet me and see me off, holding Ignatka in her arms, with Gleb standing by her, his lips trembling. He couldn't bear it, and sobbed that he didn't want me to go away. Scared by his cry, the baby also gave a thin screech. Completely broken up, I ran down the steps, hearing the heart-wrenching voices of the two children, afraid to hear a third crying voice in addition to theirs.

"What's wrong with you, damn it!" I cursed; the car door slammed, and forgetting to turn on the headlights, I tore through the yard in complete darkness. When I switched on the lights, I saw a dog running and looking around in terror. I slammed on the brakes, the car skidded, I frantically spun the steering wheel in the opposite direction, and pressing the accelerator, I shot out onto the empty street.

Half an hour later, I had calmed down a little, but the road was awful; the constantly falling snow was wet and immediately congealed into ice on the windshield.

Once every half hour I forced myself to stop, ventured out into the nasty, cold darkness, and scraped the frozen snow off the parts of the windscreen that the constantly crawling windscreen wipers could not reach.

There were no officers at the checkpoints, and there were increasingly fewer cars coming in the opposite direction. I was overtaken several times, and I stepped on the gas so as to drive in company with someone, unobtrusively staying one hundred meters or so behind. But soon these cars turned off to the left or the right, to the villages alongside the roads, and in the end I found myself alone, among the snow and the Middle Russian plateau, on the way from Nizhny Novgorod to a Ryazan village.

Sometimes I started talking out loud, but the conversation didn't catch on, and I fell silent.

You remember how Grama brought you tea in the morning, and biscuits with country butter… You woke up and drank, warm and happy…

I don't remember.

You remember.

I tried to perk myself up, to stop myself from being sad, from drowsing off or moping painfully and drearily.

Remember: you are a child. I am a child. And your body is still weak and stupid. My body. Remember…

Gramma is nearby, she loves me without measure, she is attentive and tender. And around me the world, which I measure with small steps, still believing that as soon as I grow up I will walk across it in its entirety.

Grama and I talked a lot, she played with me and sang to me, and I also loved her very much; but everything that I remembered so vividly suddenly feel apart from some reason, not a single happy event from the recent past became living and warm, and with a screech the wipers dispersed the memories from the windscreen.

The road wound through the Murom woods.

There were endless little creeks covered with ice, and villages without a single light burning.

I wanted to see at least a street light – so that it would wink in welcome – but who needed streetlights here but me.

The car travelled smoothly, although the road, I could see and feel, was slippery, uncleared and not sprinkled with sand.

After several hours I came to an intersection – my path was cut off by a four-lane highway. And here at last I saw a massive truck coming from the left, and I was happy to see it, because I wasn't lost on this frozen earth alone – here was a trucker going full speed ahead.

His truck is empty, and so he's not scared of the traffic cops or the devil, and perhaps he's also happy to see me…

This is what I thought as I pressed on the breaks to let the truck past, but the road did not hold my car, and the wheels did not grip the asphalt. And even the wind, it seemed, was blowing into the back windscreen, pushing me, placing my body, locked in a warm and smoky salon, under a blow.

Ivau! Ga!

Good morning, Papa…

I tore at the gearstick, shifting from neutral into second, then right into first – trying to brake that way. The car jolted, for a moment it seemed that it had slowed down, but I was already on the highway, and was looking stupidly ahead, into the emptiness and the falling of white snowflakes. From the left, my face, a mad-eyed reflection in the rear vision mirror, was bathed in a ghastly light.

The driver didn't slow down, but turned the wheel and powerfully moved into the empty opposing lane. The truck, crashing and waving the enormous tail of the trailer, drove right past my eyes, maybe just half a meter from my car.

When the huge hulk disappeared, stirring up a cloud of snow, I realized that I was still swaying slowly. And I was gently moving the wheel, like a child pretending to be a driver.

I crossed the road in first gear. The trucker drove in the opposing lane for about a hundred meters, then moved back into his own lane, without stopping, to tell me that I… That I was mortal.

I cracked open the window and moved into second gear. Then into third, and almost straight away into fourth.

The White Square

"Hi, Zakharka. You've aged."

We were playing hide-and-seek in the empty lot behind the shop, a few village boys.

The one whose turn it was to lead stood facing the door, loudly counting to one hundred. During this time, everyone was supposed to hide.

The dark-faced, gap-toothed, sharp-shouldered boys hid in the labyrinths of the nearby new two-story building, which smelt of brick dust, and in the dark corners, of urine. Someone sneezed in bushes, revealing himself. Others, scraping the skin on their rubs, crawled through the gap in the fence that separated the village school from the lot. And they also climbed trees and hurtled off the branches, running to overtake the leader to the door of the village shop, to touch the square drawn on it with a brick, shouting "Keep away!"

Because if you didn't say that, you'd have to be the leader yourself.

I was the smallest one, so no one really looked for me.

But I took care to hide, I lay there motionless, and listened to the toothy laughter of the boys, quietly envying their impudence, their swift heels and dirty language. Their dirty language was made of different letters than the ones I pronounced: when they cursed, each word rang out and jumped like a small and ferocious ball. When I cursed – secretly, in a whisper, with my face in the grass; or loudly, in an empty house when my mother was at work – the words nastily hung on my lips, and all I had to do was wipe them off with my sleeve, and then for a long time examine what had dried on it…

I watched the boy who was "it" from the grass, sharp-eyed as a gopher. When he went to the other side, I gave what I thought was a loud Cossack's whoop, and trotted on my short legs to the door of the village shop, with an unnatural smile that seemed to be made of plasticine on my face, and in my heart a feeling of unusual triumph. The boy who was It lazily turned his head for a moment in my direction, and didn't even stop, as if I wasn't running to the door, but that something stupid, obtrusive and pointless had happened.

But I honestly carried my smile and the unceasing triumph to the white square on the door, and hit it with such force that my palm burnt, and I shouted out "keep away!"

(Keep away, away, my life – I'm already here, by the door, and beating my hands on it)

After I shouted, I heard, not without pleasure, laughter behind my back – so someone had appreciated how I jumped so nimbly, how I ran over…

"Oh…" I said more loudly than I needed to, and turned around self-satisfied, showing for all to see that I was tired from running. And of course, I immediately saw that it wasn't me, naked-bellied, who delighted people. Sashka had behaved strangely again.

"I've aged. You age particularly fast when you start to look for justifications from life."

"But when you believe your own justifications yourself, then it's easier."

"How can I not believe them, Sasha? What should I do then?"

Sasha doesn't listen to me. He never comes. And I don't know where he is.

"Sasha, what can I say even if I do come?"

He has a frozen face with turned out lips and frost-covered cheek-bones, resembling the body of a frozen bird; he has no facial expressions.

"It's cold, Zakharka... Cold and stifling..." he says, not listening to me.

Sashka was unusual. He had a blonde forelock, a face of tender beauty, always ready to break out into a thoughtful, sensitive smile. He was kind to us little boys, not telling us what to do, not saying disgustingly vulgar things, never swearing. He remembered each one by name and asked: "How are things?" He shook hands in a manly way. The heart leapt towards him.

He allowed himself to laugh at the local crooked-faced and crooked-legged hooligans – the Chebryakov brothers. He looked at them with narrowed eyes, without taking the smile off his face. The Chebryakovs were twins, a year older than Sashka. In childhood that's a big difference. At least it is for boys.

I heard him laughing once – the only one among the rest of us, who did not even dare to crack a smile – when Chebryakov climbed up a tree and tore the sleeve of his shirt to the armpit, with a loud tearing sound.

Sashka laughed, and his laugh was unforced and merry.

"What you laughing for?" said Chebryakov, one of the brothers, forgetting about his sleeve. His pupils constantly moved from left to right, as if he couldn't decide to stop at Sasha's smile. "What you laughing for?"

"Are you forbidding me to?" Sasha asked.

All my life I've looked for an excuse to say that – like Sashka. But when there was an excuse, I didn't have the strength to say it, and I would get into a fight, so as not to become completely frightened. All my life I looked for an excuse to say that – and I couldn't find one, but he could – at the age of nine.

Sashka mocked the movement of Chebryakov's pupils with his cheerful eyes, and it seemed to me that no one but me noticed, because all the rest were looking away.

Chebryakov spat.

Oh, these childish, youthful, manly gobs of spit! A sign of nervousness, a sign that the self-control is running out – and if they can't now become hysterical and bare their claws, and can't release the white spit touching the corners of their lips, and reveal their young fangs, then things will never work out again.

Chebryakov spat, and squatted down suddenly. He raised his arm with the torn sleeve, and looked at it, whispering something and interspersing the words with curses addressed only to the sleeve.

"It's stuffy, Zakharka. I feel stifled." I can hardly tell what he is saying from his icy, almost motionless lips. He has no voice.

"Maybe you're thirsty. I have something in the fridge…"

"No!" he shouts, almost spitting. And I'm afraid that the shout will split his face in two – like the carcass of a frozen bird breaks, revealing red and tangled insides.

Goats wandered around the village during the daytime, I remember that Sasha's grandmother also had them. Sasha's grandmother lived in our village, and his parents lived in the neighboring one. Sashka spent the nights here and there, and returned home through the forest, in the evening.

I sometimes imagined that I was walking with him, and he was holding my little paw in his firm grip, it was dark but I wasn't scared.

Yes, the goats wandered around, and bleated stupidly, and scratched their horns on the fences. Sometimes they ran towards you, lowering their stupid, wooden heads – at the last moment, hearing the clatter, you would turn around, and clumsily lifting your legs, you would throw back your white boyish head, throw a frightened sideways glance, and run, run run – but still you would get a not very painful, but very insulting butt, and tumble to the ground. After this, the goat would immediately lose interest in the fallen person, and run off, bleating.

The she goats were interested in the boys' games. When they discovered you in the bushes, they would shudder, shake their heads, and complain to the billy goat: *Someone's ly-y-y-y-ing here!* The billy goat pretended not to hear. Then the she goats would come closer. Their nostrils flared and their teeth were bared. *E-e-e-i!* they cried stupidly in your face.

There's no wolf to get you… you would think, offended.

The nanny goats also wandered over to us in the empty lot, hearing the racket and the rich boyish laughter. Sometimes the laughter died down – when the boy who was It started to search – and the goats wandered around perplexed, looking for the person who had been making the noise. They found Sashka.

Sashka sat with his back to a tree, sometimes cawing in response to the crow which was startled by our games, and which had its nest not far away. He cawed skillfully and mockingly, which seemed to annoy the crow even more. Sashka's cawing amused the boys, and they revealed themselves to the boy who was It by their laughter.

A nanny goat also took an interest in the "crow" sitting under the tree, and was immediately mounted and grabbed by the horns.

Sashka emerged from his hiding place on the goat's back, pushing his heels off the ground, shouting "Keep away!" and whooping merrily.

It was getting dark and cold, and the boys didn't want to continue the games anymore. They were already tired of hiding and, bored and cold in the dry grass by the gap in the fence, or on the cooling bricks of the new building, they slowly went home, to the steamed milk, a tired mother and a slighty drunken father.

One of the Its, tired of looking for older boys, found me – right away, easily, barely after counting to one hundred, he went straight to my hiding place with an easy step.

"Go on," he nodded casually.

And I started to look for the boys.

I wandered through the bushes, raising my thin legs high as the nettles lashed me, and white nettle welts appeared on my ankles, and the chill sent grainy goose bumps crawling like ants down my back.

I sniveled and noticed someone slowly climbing down a tree and calmly walking away as I approached – home, home... And I didn't dare to shout.

"Hey, what's with you, guys..." I whispered bitterly, as if I had been left alone on the frontline. "Hey, what's with you..."

The crow fell silent, and the nanny goats were driven home.

I walked through the village, past the school with its sad yellow sides, shedding fine flakes of peeling plaster. The janitor was smoking by the school, and the tiny light flickered.

It flickered like a heart that was pumping blood for the last time.

The cigarette butt flew into the grass, flashing bright red.

I returned to the village shop, stumbling ove stones on the dark road, already trembling and chattering with my remaining milk teeth. The white square on the door could not be made out.

"Keep away," I said in a whisper and placed my palm to the place where the square had been.

"I've come home, Sasha."

"I called you."

"Sasha, I can't stand this, share it with me."

"No, Zakharka".

At home, my mother washed me, in a basin with warm, foamy water.

"We played hide and seek, Mama."

"Did they find you?"

"No. Just once."

Tea and yellow butter, cold as if it had been cut out of a patch of sunlight on the morning water. I'll have another sandwich. And more milk in my tea.

"Mama, I want to tell you about the game."

"Just a second, son."

And another glass of tea. And three sugar cubes.

"Where are you going, Mama? I want to tell you now..."

But she's gone.

Then I'll build a house with the sugar cubes.

Sashka's parents thought that he had gone to stay with his grandma. His grandma thought that he had gone home to his parents. There were no telephones in the country back then, no one rang anyone.

He hid in a fridge – an empty freezing chamber that stood by the village shop. A battered cable led from the shop to the fridge.

The fridge didn't open from the inside.

They looked for Sasha for two days, and his grandma came to me. I didn't know what to say to her. The Chebryakovs were summoned to the police station.

Early Monday morning, Sashka was found by the school janitor.

The boy had pushed his arms and legs against the door of the fridge. Tears were frozen on his face. His square mouth, showing a bitten-through, icy tongue, was open.

In other words…
Poems by Zakharka

*

In the treetops the dew
is beating its wings,
the breathing greenery
lowers its face,
the blackness of wet
berries lightly drowses –
rains have rocked them
to sleep in their cradle.

In the reflection through eyelids
cracked open, half waking,
there was a mist; and the earth,
and damp berries,
and the grass underfoot,
pockmarked from cold,
caressed me, pretending
to be the Homeland.

* * *

I've already lived more than once,
but I dare not live any longer.
Either sensual passion
or a foolish idea
to live it out hindered me
from gathering up the rest of the crumbs.
And sweet snow fondled
the roads of fir.

Forgive me, father, that
I had no desire
to catch with my hot mouth
the last breath.
The gift of fate, alas,
I did not preserve, or show it affection,
and did not hold life
by its slippery wrists.

Without lamentation or rage,
I fell to earth unripe.
The soul yet once more
easily said farewell to the body.
Speech cannot contain
the time and distance
from such short meetings
and frequent partings.

I've lived so often, that
I forgot places and dates.
and to recall all that
makes no sense here.
In the world wars
I didn't manage to age –
I perished in two of them
And I will be there for the third.

* * *

As fingernails grow after death,
so my feeling for you,
with all the undernail dirt
when life's time span runs out
will not stop its motion.

Do not fear – if the autumn is long,
it will not be eternal;
in fact,
this is just what you have to fear.

December with disfigured face,
and I with icy hands,
And you mixed up in the scent of lilacs,
and with hair the color of wet cherries,
and with other trash,
other junk,
other lies.

* * *

I wanted a cure – too late:
the cough and the cold disappeared.
I'll call my puppy Bismark,
and pour champagne on the asters.
The path to madness lies close
in January's dry midday.

The snows on the fir trees have ripened.
Shall we knock them down tonight?
It's so inexpressibly charming
to look at your legs,
that if one looks past them,
one loses the meaning of vision.

You must have got better,
I don't remember you this way.
If I couldn't know at all, but it's too late.

And if you press your palms
to your eyes, and removing them, look
at the stars – they are like chandeliers.

I mixed all the lines up – what for.
You might just as well
tangle your shoelaces up.
Can't sleep. In the nooks of the brain
it's all you; and, counting the minutes,
I lose the count only toward morning…

Failed sonnet

You walked round.
I walked through.
Whispering of feelings,
I hurt my jaw.
I fired shots (here's the rhyme:
without aiming).

You walked in the middle.
I turned the corner.
All feelings are simple:
pencil or charcoal.
Sporadic simplicity –
I was scaring off pride.

But is there a point weaving
speeches about this!
When your hands touched my neck
less often in autumn than my scarf,
from where came the hope
that the rivers would freeze in the winter?

All feelings are simple.
Only poses are complex.
We lived through autumn
to the white payoff.
And the frosts have a scent – of frost.
And the color of rain was terribly rainy.

* * *

I have still lost
the value of my words
so often admitting
dead
made-up
stillborn feelings –
lost them
for which I was punished
by solitude
in another icy january
by salt
by an empty horizon
by snow
by the husky voice
of solitude
depression's unkempt goblin
misery's green corner

words are all quite
worthless

never mind

tomorrow morning
a girl with a lazy smile
will look at me in the tram
she won't like me
but something will interest her

before she leaves the tram
she'll turn around again
and our eyes will meet

outside
catching up with her
I'll say
in my home there are many boring books
I also have handcuffs
and some money for a bottle of beer
I'm a poet and also I can
play Vertinsky on the guitar
(your fingers smell of incense)
I can play something about your fingers

* * *

I still hope: like a child
who breaks a vase and freezes in horror
wishing it would come together
by itself and go back to the sideboard.

Reading books, I still dream
and still believe that life
and death will sort things out
and I – alone – will be left innocent.

I still hope. And hope
does not soothe me,
but slightly embitters me.

* * *

and at the slave market in Ancient Rome
where the smell makes you sick
at the noisy, savage market
the son of a patrician
eccentric and conceited
I wander with my slave boy

and you are there
in the crowd of slaves for sale
dirty and angry
you turn away and close your eyes
but I saw you two thousand years later
I recognized you at once

and bought by me
you are the only one who has the right
to come to me in the mornings
when I am still asleep
you bring me berries and juices
and of all imaginable grief on earth
I am only tormented by one
when a cherry stone
gets caught in my front teeth

White dreams

July was swarthy,
but August was white,
and dreams were white.
The whole earth turned pale or grey,
as though it had eaten henbane.
And we felt uneasy
because of all this whiteness.

White as a ghost,
covered with a sheet,
you slept, curled up like a cat,
and waking up, charmingly angry,
sent curses to mosquitoes,
amusing and obscene.

In sleep your head was spinning
and so was something older.
You barely breathed,
thrashing the bed without mercy,
blowing away yesterday's narcosis
with your breath.

Your hand called out for mine,
like a bird looks for food,
like dried-out grass craves rain,
I gave my hand, although you slept,
you intertwined your palm in mine
tenderly and lightly.

Burnt by you into ashes
I got used to the quivering of eyes.
In love with you – in a swampy mire,
in your love – in the heavenly heights.
And in the lines of fate and life
our sweat trickled down.

From the wind the censer smoke
entered the open window.
And birds walked on the tables
and drank our wine.

* * *

I lost my matches.
I lost the box, I say.
I lost the feeling of frailty,
the fatality of being.
Insolent as a weed,
I stand in the wet wind.
Happiness, how huge you are.
Where can I hide you?
I have no sense of cold or slush.
The shroud of the wind,
the mist and snow don't reach me.

Something crumbles in my hands.
It seems to be winter:
it rages, but cannot be heard,
like a silent film.

I don't take it to heart.
I will not learn to do so.
I want so to accept it,
but my heart, like that puppy,
sits foolishly in the corner,
in the puddle on the floor.
It licks its belly or scratches
its cheekbone.

Heart, where are you, what are you?
Are you nowhere?
I don't know your beating,
I don't feel your heaviness.
Lord, stern God,
how did you not guess,
That I stand here, smiling.
Even that I simply stand.
There is no feeling of time.
Warm, mad, alive,
I see nothing but happiness.
Why do I need so much of it.

Cold, I know, it's cold.
I know this and cannot
let even an atom
of the black azure into me –
the evening reeking of smoke –
the city in dirty snow –
the deadliness of this heart –
the sound of this wind.

I no longer know
how to pardon or reprove.
What should I ask God for?
Nothing more than a smoke.

* * *

If, on the train,
sitting opposite each other,
we press our cheeks
to the frozen glass,
and
we try to join our lips,
a butterfly will be left
on the glass,
and
on our cheeks the pattern
of fingers of everyone
who wanted to know
where we're going.

* * *

I know not what I do,
I talk of love to you.
Red blinking from each traffic light.
Upon this foul and evil night
Continents sink into the deep
How am I supposed to sleep…

Each traffic light is flashing.
I ignore an obstacle to the right,
I ignore entire chapters.
And this book has no end.
In a daze, I drive into the ditch…

There is blinking red… scarlet…
dark pink… fiery…
Like a heart, the cars stop moving.
A pale moon, like a sentry,

the scorched shadow of a willow…
Let them know that I'm alive.

I know not what I do,
I talk of love to you.
You are my dear, my only one,
You've been my wife a thousand years.

Dance

Robins in scarlet clothes.
Mowers in white shirts.
Pain in work-worn joints.
Burning in maddened arms.

The mowers have taken off their clothes,
their bodies are blue with cold.
Sails have grown upon
the masts of pines and aspens.

I drink the salty juice of fatigue,
I feel no sickness, and no ease.
Groggy, half-asleep I walk
barefoot across the sunset.

If you are barefoot, go and dance,
until your heels are burning.
The mowers, naked to the waist,
burn robins in the sunset.

* * *

Stenka Razin
lazily watched the bustle of the bees
bees swarmed around his head
with burnt eyelashes
and honey juice on his skin

the bees swarmed
around his head mounted on a stake

so much like a flower
like a flower on a stem

* * *

Boys to the right – to hell with them.
Girls to the left – where the heart is.

The squadron roars to tear an aorta,
the mother brings drink to the hall.

The roasted rooster pecked
where childhood
played, and beat its wings.

We cannot get away from the dead.
Who's last in line to heaven –
I'm after you.

Sky full of drizzle, thoughts full
of heresy, in a day
or two the mass will be held here

Your eye-socket or jaw
will be preserved
by river slime, a nasty father,
the last refuge.

With every beat of the rooster's wings
the unknown darkness is revealed.

Mother brings us something to drink,
The pitcher beats, as in a fever,
against the teeth.

* * *

woozy
on tired horses
in the scents of uneasy July sun
damp cloth and sweat
we enter the village

the frightened peasants
bring us food
knowing already
that their baron is now
to be hanged
(who yesterday cried:
to the stables! –
and today: wasn't I like
a father to you!)
hanged by the rib
hanged on the gates

and the uncomprehending peasants
cross themselves and hide
the girls in the haylofts
not knowing that the freedom

given to them
cannot be bought with hospitality

and they do not guess that by evening
the girls will come running in terror
from the haylofts that we set alight
and we will cool them
with buckets of water from the well

and from the heat and the screaming
our timid horses will shudder
and the chief will dress us down
tomorrow for our debauchery

but the blaze will be seen
from as far away as Astrakhan

* * *

Plunging their nails in blood,
the entire dense army howls.
Butchery until night
or fighting since morning.
The heavy mist, like a monster,
looks greedily into our eyes.
And the desert does not heed.
What can it say anyway.
Dazed friends draw off
tremulous mead.
From the beauties in the district
only death takes it in the mouth.
You cannot find a ram, or new gates.
It's too early to retreat.
And no one wants to advance.
We sit here. Scratch our ribs.
Twist our mouths. Wait
for an order.
Golden trash! Guys!
God remembers us!
Here's our angel in the sky.
But he is squint-eyed.
The sun shines so brightly…
like a fool without pants.

Will we make it or is it doubtful?
Hey, toss a coin.

From the cloudy blue a white scarf waves.

... You know what's her name
how we wandered barefoot
and swum naked
we were caught in the rapids…

I know it all, brother.

* * *

sometimes I think:
perhaps everything happened
otherwise and what is happening now
is just tatters of post-traumatic delirium
a spatter of ruptured memory
idle running of suspended reason

maybe that spring
lying with a machine gun
in the frozen and revolting mud
covered with cartridge shells
maybe then – three hours later –
when the shots died down
and everyone wandered
over to the column
torn apart like a bag

of Christmas presents
I did not get up and remained
lying, already freezing
and twisted, they dragged me
into the vehicle
and to tear the gun out
of my hands they braced their leg
against my hard stomach
but I didn't care
or maybe
in that winter accident
I did not look indifferently
at the intricate patterns
of the windscreen
and remained sitting
with the driver who had
driven into my ribcage
with stupidly open mouth
and staring eyes

but most likely in the village
where I was born and
where I haven't been
for so long –
if I can get in there unnoticed
and end up there somehow as a spy
hiding behind the trees by a yellow
ridiculous building –
in that village I will see

a fair-haired boy
with skinny arms
looking at baby chicks
who of course is not me
and cannot be me

* * *

I'll buy myself a portrait of Stalin
three by three
in the storeroom of a museum
closed for repairs forever
from the janitor,
who remembers nothing.
Doesn't even remember Stalin.

I'll buy a portrait of Stalin. – Pipe, coat, cunning squint. – A cheap whore will buy Rublyov. – Bow to the ground and weep. – All sluts can be bought with dope. – They will all stuff their cheeks with pity. – Baddies, your mama, turncoats. – I'll gouge out your eyes, tyrants. – These are dying, these are frozen. – Are these the lands you inhabit.

Impenitent in the ruins. – Ancestor of my lost grandchildren. – From the fires of the holy Russian camp. – I'll buy myself a portrait of Stalin. – Even a tyrant, even a devil. – I'll exchange it for a cross and an amulet. – I'll be a scum, you'll dream of me. – Hello, motherland! We are your herd.

We are your cattle and your flock. – We will cook a dish for you. – From two thousand years of fearlessness. – Eat it, dog! paid for with blood! – Our granary is looted. – A grey roof slides sideways. – Our gates are unassailable. – They were torn like a mouth by a yawn. Your lover ogles-Gogols you. – My Dostoevsky homeland – the cornea of the deer's eye. – Fierce dogs have torn your guts out.

Hey, icon-painting sluts! Raise your shamelessness, your crimson skirts. – Your eyes, tired as God. – Your foolish ginger heads. – Hey, My Rublyov poets, how much heresy there is in you. – My down-to-earth girls, my reckless boys.

Pavel Vasiliev

Artyom Vesyoly

Ivan Pribludny

Boris Kornilov

Come to me, my friends. – We'll eat black berries together. – I ask you for understanding. – I bring you a request for mercy from my heavenly district. – Your names are in my name. – Our motherland is our protectress. – Eyes up and keep the music quieter – the day of commemoration begins.

I'll buy myself a portrait of Stalin…

* * *

the sound of a bell
the scent of flowers
you
dancing a waltz alone
on a hill
your legs are so alluring

I dreamt the most radiant dream
in a rickety truck
where I was lost among
the corpses of people
who were shot along with me

Concert

In the midnight heat at a café
by the Jordan
everything was mixed.
The cocktail did not cool.
Faces were touched
with inspired heat:
the explosive wave was
as soft as sour cream.
The head trembles.
Where do we attack?
The East is scattered.
Borders are everywhere.
Everything was mixed.
And the machine gun is pitiful.
The brain is squashed with terror,
like a tomato.
O, spine of mine,
I cannot flee from you!

Above the ocean troubles have begun,
their step rattles like a happy skeleton.
Here midnight is beaten by exquisite rockets,
their crimson gullet raised to the Almighty.
But He does not grant a cry nor a sigh.
The infantry tears ribcages in a roar,
and lets hearts go free, enraged.

And the funeral songs of the East.
And the thin throats of rockets in the dawn.

Stay away from the flash of cigarettes:
here snipers don't believe in glowworms.
Where's that Semite who asked us a question?
The answer's ready, please come in after three
glasses. Boy, give us a pomegranate.
And a knife – to cut it into pieces,
and a dish to gather the crimson juice.
Allah Aqbar, O my little counterpart!
Let us break this vulgar omnipotence.

Sunrise. The East is losing its boundaries.
Ripping off the skin, it is sweet to discover
the rye meat. Here the fat is layered.
I stamp my foot: East, reveal your soul to me!
Can it really be a pathetic gap?
Inside Saddam the wind seeks its echo.
Inside Adam it is muffled, like in the earth.
But at Sodom a blunder appears
in a hat with earflaps, and shows a tipsy face.

Be afraid then, haggard neurotic,
the quiet heel will squash you.
And there will be peace.
And blossoming will come into the world.
We will see crooked caterpillars in the flowers.
The gloom of trousers will impassively arise,
without distinguishing the guilty
and the innocent.
Meanwhile we are still a little tipsy.
The East hangs like a curtain in Israeli cafes.
We listen to a recording from Palestine.

Meat concert in the café by the Jordan…

* * *

…better to make a hole in the snowy
crust with rusty spit,
to whisper with your face in the snow:
"well, you've fired your shots, soldier…",
not to call the ones who have gone
to the height, where our
piece of land was taken and appropriated,

and better, squinting, to see a furious flag,
softening like honey in the sky,
and hear the step of unseen phalanxes,
the phalanx of the finger touching the trigger,

and better to fondle and caress your trouble
your troublesome, but proper victory,

feeding on nasty anger, and in delirium
to carry into Thursday what repelled
you on Wednesday –

there, Father, there is the Fatherland, that's all;
there is no more meaning here, no answer,

fallen leaves, weeds of the steppe
misery baked from age to age.

For you the Empire stinks, and we are the serfs
Of the Empire, we are its dust and smoke,
We are its salt, and every two meters
We sanctify her Highness with ourselves.

There is a salty taste here, here at dawn
rye blood rises up to the heavens,
earthly forgetfulness dances with us
from "so far" to "urgently,"

here the heavens are big-bellied,
their undercoat
is slimy and musty, it does not warm,
but steams,
here every unrepentant teenager
is nastily tongue-tied.

Here our tongues are frozen,
our stomachs, each
eyelash, each hair,

we are all nameless, but every fallen one
sits among us at the gloomy table.

So, it is better – better, as we are,
as we were, and as we will be,
here are the ribs – to protect the heart,
here is the cross,
here are the painful crossroads
of the homeland,

and I would rather have its vastness
than your bending, calculating,
gossip, budgets,
your smirks, nasty lies,
futile words and false victories…

* * *

Forgetfulness. I don't remember childhood,
the order of numbers, the writing of words…
My softened heart
has outgrown me for good.

I searched for you, looked out for news,
I followed you into the wilderness, and there
the branches that you pushed aside
hit me so sweetly in the eyes.

The Sergeant

He had this conversation with every soldier in the unit, and more than once.

He looked like a normal guy, but you never can tell.

"Every person must determine certain things for themselves," he said for the umpteenth time, and the Sergeant already guessed what he was talking about. He listened languidly, not without secret irony. "I know what I will never allow myself to do," he said – his name was Vitka. "And I consider this to be correct. And I know what I'll never allow my woman, my wife to do. I'll never use her mouth. And I won't allow her to do this to herself, even if she wants to. And I'll never use her…"

"You already said that, Vitya," the Sergeant interrupted him. "I remember where you won't do her… I'm even prepared to share your point of view. But why do you keep telling everyone about this?"

"No, you do agree that if you commit such acts, that means that you degrade yourself, and your woman?" Vitka said, getting excited.

The Sergeant realized that he had put his foot in it, and that now he would either have to lie, or argue about a stupid topic.

Should he tell Vitka what he would do right now with his beloved woman…

"Why don't you tell me, Vitya, why you didn't charge the walkie-talkies?" the Sergeant changed the subject.

Vitka knitted his brows and tried to go out of the semi-darkness of the post onto the street, where it was just becoming light.

"No, you wait, Vitya," the Sergeant said, stirring up the already fading mood. "Why did you take half-dead radios? Why didn't you charge the batteries?"

Vitya was silent.

"I told you three times: 'Charge them! Check them! Charge them!' the Sergeant continued, sneering and enjoying himself. You answered three times: 'I charged them! I checked them! Everything's fine!'"

"But there was enough to last almost till morning," Vitya justified himself.

"Almost until morning! They croaked at three a.m.! What if something had happened?"

"What could happen…" Vitya replied quietly, but in a tone that was meant not to irritate: a conciliatory tone.

The Sergeant was not in fact irritated enough to answer. He himself… didn't really believe…

Their unit had been stationed in this strange, hot place by a mountainous border for a month now. The guys were going mad in their male loneliness and sweaty boredom. There was nowhere to swim. They had driven to the nearest village a few times in a jeep and only seen goats, fat women and a few old people.

But the village shop and the pharmacy looked almost the same way that they did in distant, quiet and secluded Russia. The guys bought all sorts of crunchy and salty rubbish, and spat the shells of nuts and salty saliva out of the window as they drove back.

The base was ten minutes' drive from the village. It was a strange building... They probably planned to make a club here, but got sick of building it and abandoned it.

They slept there, ate, slept again, then furiously pumped iron, swelling up their crimson backs and blue veins. They resembled invigorated animals, smelt of animals, and laughed like wolves.

They wandered around the area to begin with, with the officers, of course. They looked around.

A guy nicknamed Sluggish stepped on a snake and called everyone over to look it.

"It's poisonous," Sluggish said in a satisfied tone.There were pigment marks visible on his cheekbones. The snake angrily hissed and writhed with its nasty little head against the tip of the boot, and Sluggish laughed. He squashed its head with his other boot and cut the snake in half with a fearfully sharp knife. He raised his foot, and the tail danced a finale.

After the guys had fired shots out of the gun slits and the posts, they were forbidden to make noise and fire shots. But they really wanted to shoot a bit more. To imagine an attack of bearded devils from the other side of the mountains, from the border, and repel this attack, disperse it and break it up.

They had three posts, two useless ones and another on a stony and dusty path from that black, strange side, where angry separatists lived.

Today the guys were stationed at the post located by the road. Here there was stationary radar, but the guys on the shift before last had done something stupid: the idiots had probably got drunk, and dropped it, or fallen on it from above. So it didn't work. The radar operator was supposed to come here first thing in the morning to fix it.

Sluggish looked into the dispersing darkness. The Sergeant was prepared to swear that Sluggish's nostrils were trembling, and that his pigmented cheek was shaking. Sluggish wants to tear someone to pieces. He came here to kill a person, at least one, and he did not even hide this desire. "It would be great to see a human head flying apart," he said, smiling.

"Sluggish, do you plan to stay at this post long?" the Sergeant asked him sometimes.

"Why not stay here," Sluggish replied without a question mark, without emotions, and touched the walls, the rough concrete. It seemed to him that the concrete was eternal, that he himself was eternal, and that the game could only be in his favor, because how could it be otherwise.

At seven in the morning, half past seven at the latest, they were supposed to be relieved by the next shift, and the Sergeant, lying on top of the sleeping bag, with a cigarette in his hand, looked at the clock. He felt like a hot meal, there was probably borshch at the base... Today was Wednesday, so there would be borshch.

Smoking made him feel ill, because he was hungry. The smoke dispersed in the semi-darkness.

There were six of them; the others were Ginger, Ridge and Samara.

Samara, the youngest of them, had served in Samara; Ginger was bald, and why he was called Ginger no one remembered, and he didn't talk about it himself; Ridge was short and had a strange, amazing strength, which he used in unusual ways; he was constantly bending or crushing something, just for fun.

The Sergeant – everyone called him Sergeant – sometimes wished that Ridge would fight Sluggish, it would be interesting to see how it ended up, but they avoided each other. Even when they ate stewed meat out of cans, they sat at a distance from each other, so their elbows wouldn't hit accidentally.

Sluggish fished through the backpack, looking for something to eat; he was hungry too, and in general was constantly eating, persistently moving his pigmented cheekbones.

Ridge, on the other hand, ate little, as if reluctantly; it seemed as if could go without food altogether.

When Sluggish was hungry, he became aggressive and picky. He would constantly bug someone, and really wanted to make jokes besides, but was not always able to do so.

"Vitya," he said. "Why did you come here?"

"I love my Homeland," Vitya replied.

Sluggish choked.

"Fuck me," he said. "What Homeland?"

Vitya shrugged his shoulders, as if to say, that's a stupid question.

"You can love your Homeland at home, you understand, Vitya?" Sluggish found a piece of bread and started tearing off pieces of it with his fingers, nibbling on it. "But to come here to love your Homeland – that's perverse. Worse than taking it in the mouth, you understand?"

"So you're a pervert?" Vitya asked.

"Of course," Sluggish agreed. "And Samara's a pervert. Look at how he sleeps: like a pervert…"

"I'm not asleep," Samara replied, without opening his eyes.

"You hear what he said: '*I'm not asleep,*'" Sluggish remarked. "But he agrees with the first part of my statement. And the Sergeant's also a pervert."

Sluggish looked at the Sergeant, hoping that he would keep up the joke.

The Sergeant stubbed out a cigarette against the wall, and because he had nothing better to do, he immediately lit a second. He didn't respond to Sluggish's glance.

He couldn't remember when he had last pronounced this word – *Homeland*. There hadn't been one for a long time. At some point, maybe in his youth, his Homeland had disappeared, and in its place nothing had formed. And nothing was needed.

Sometimes there was a forgotten, crushed, childish, painful feeling beating in his heart. The sergeant didn't admit it and didn't respond. Who hadn't felt this…

And now he thought a little, and then stopped.

The Homeland – people don't think about it. There are no thoughts about the Homeland. You don't think about your mother – not chance images from your childhood, but thoughts. In the army, it seemed shameful when other people talked about their mothers, that she… I don't know what she did… cooked soup, made pies, kissed them on the forehead. Is this something you can say aloud? And in front of these unshaven men. It's even embarrassing to think it to yourself.

It was only possible to think seriously about what scared Vitya. Although here it was also better to get a grip.

…He'd become nervous again…

Sometimes, the Sergeant recalled, once every few years, he would start to feel a strange nakedness, as though he had shed his skin. Then it was easy to offend him.

The first time, as a teenager, when this feeling seized him, he felt discouraged and humiliated and hid at home, he didn't go to school, he knew that any idiot could upset him and go unpunished.

Later, when he was grown up, he was so afraid of this intermittent weakness that he started drinking vodka – and barely got out of that.

The last time this morbid feeling came was when his children were born, two boys.

And then the Sergeant fled from this feeling, which suddenly gained new shades and became almost intolerable. He fled here, to the post.

Essentially, the Sergeant now realized, this feeling came down to the fact that he no longer had the right to die when he felt like it.

It turned out that he needed to look after himself. How humiliating this was for a man…

The Sergeant, who had never seriously valued his life, was suddenly surprised by his evident weakness. Humans are such laughable creatures, he thought, looking at the guys pumping iron. This hunk of meat, with so many bones, and it just needed a few grams of lead… why even lead – a thin needle would be enough if it went in deeply…

To live to the full extent of his power, restricting himself in everything, to sleep little and eat almost nothing – the Sergeant could do all of this without difficulty. Furthermore, he never saw any special value in human freedom, rather believing it to be shameful. Various unpleasant people had talked about freedom so often recently, but when he listened to them, the Sergeant was almost certain that when they said *freedom,* they meant something else. The color of their faces, perhaps…

No one said that the most terrifying lack of freedom was the inability to make the main choice easily, and not a lack of a few indulgences in vulgar trifles, which actually came down to the right to wear stupid rags, go out dancing at night, and then not work during the day, and if you did work, then the devil knew at what, for what and why.

Recently the Sergeant had made a choice: it seemed to him that he had. He had, he believed, managed to claw out the right not to look after himself, and left.

But now he lay there, feeling the cold of the concrete dust with his shoulder, and felt longing – not for anyone, but an empty, sluggish sense of longing without any attachment. Nothing was happening.

No one was even coming to collect them.

"What's the time, Sergeant?" Samara asked, without opening his eyes.

"It's after eight," the Sergeant replied, without looking at the clock.

They lay there,almost calmly until ten, then became worried.

"Come on Vitya, you freak, pray now," the Sergeant began to pep himself up. "It's early to bury you yet."

Vitya didn't say anything.

"Or go climb a tree and wave your handkerchief, so they notice you from the base," Sluggish immediately joined in.

Ridge and Ginger were watching the road: they hadn't changed since they began at four in the morning.

"Sluggish, replace Ginger, it's time," the Sergeant said.

"Time for what? I've done my own duty," Sluggish replied. "Vitya can go."

Sluggish had got some idea in his head, he wanted to make some nasty joke about how Vitya should be "used", but he didn't manage to come up with anything.

"Vitya will go with you too," the Sergeant replied, and got up himself.

This was a simple psychological gesture: he didn't have to get up at all, but if you're on your feet, your team works better than from a lying position.

In any case, with animals like Sluggish, it was generally better to keep yourself in line, and stay alert. In empty deserts, subordination is sometimes forgotten.

What's going on? the Sergeant thought, walking back and forth aimlessly. *Where has everyone disappeared to... We'll soon be out of cigarettes.*

Ridge squatted down and started squashing an empty can, turning it into a pancake.

Ridge, the Sergeant recalled, was the only one in the unit who frightened the regiment's German shepherd, which was not even afraid of Sluggish, who constantly harassed it. Although Ridge did not do anything bad to it. He just started stroking its back, and then, without even noticing himself, he tried to pin it to the ground, and could not stop from playing some more: he didn't let the dog get up, he butted it, and lifted it up with his heavy hands, until the dog, with an unusual, almost hysterical squeal, shook itself loose. It then made large circles, looking sideways at Ridge with an eye that was frightened and furious at the same time. Ridge then stood without a smile, not quite sure of what had happened, and looking like a heavy, perhaps underwater, rock that would break in two any boat that happened to hit it.

"Ridge, I forgot, do you have any children?" the Sergeant asked. He suddenly thought with horror how Ridge would play with his kids.

Ridge shrugged his shoulders:

"Where from," he replied strangely.

"You ask Vitya where they come from," Sluggish joined in. "You probably don't use your girlfriend properly, you've got it all wrong."

Ridge frowningly looked to where Sluggish's voice came from – he couldn't see him behind the wall.

"So you're not married?" the Sergeant asked.

Ridge shrugged his shoulders, as if he didn't know himself whether he was married or not.

…Samara turned on his side and seemed to fall asleep. Ginger sat by the wall, pressing his bare head against it; it was strange that it didn't hurt him.

…There is no greater emptiness than waiting.

As a child, the Sergeant would try to cheer himself up at any depressing moment by telling himself: *Just imagine that you have to die today: with what melancholy you will be to remember this time that seemed completely intolerable to you… Enjoy yourself, idiot, breathe every second. How good it is to breathe…*

"I'm sick of lying around here!" Samara suddenly got up. He didn't look sleepy at all.

"What's with you? Sleep!" the Sergeant said. "You'll go back to the base and sleep anyway."

"It's different there. There I'll… sleep peacefully. But here… Did their car break down or something?"

The Sergeant did not reply.

"All three at once?" Ginger asked for him.

There were three cars in the unit.

"Maybe they went somewhere in two of them," Samara suggested.

"Where?" Ginger asked. "To Russia?"

"How do I know?" Samara said; he realized himself that there wasn't really anywhere to go.

He fell on his back once more and lay there with his eyes open.

"I feel sick," he said.

The Sergeant thought for a moment, and said the thing with which he had calmed himself at such moments, and which he had recalled recently. He generally avoided abstract conversations with the soldiers – they were pointless, but here he unexpectedly felt himself to be in a lyrical mood.

Samara looked at the Sergeant in surprise and didn't reply: he simply didn't know what to say.

"Sergeant, what did you used to do for a job?" Ginger asked.

"I was a bouncer in a bar," the Sergeant replied, turning back to Ginger.

"And after that?"

"A loader."

"And after that?"

"After that I was a bouncer again."

"That's it?"

"Yes."

"Did you ever work as a psychologist?"

"No."

"You could. Talk some sense into people."

I shouldn't have done that, no, the Sergeant decided. *I shouldn't have said all that, after all, I know...*

"All right, Ginger, I'll think about it," he replied calmly.

"I've got a name," Ginger said, half closing his eyes.

The Sergeant directed his clear gaze at him, but Ginger didn't react.

"If I understand correctly, two people will call you by this name: your mama and I," the Sergeant said.

"I have no mama."

"Well, just me then."

"Just you."

The Sergeant swallowed an angry mouthful of spit.

"Get up, private," he said to Ginger.

Ginger opened his lazy eyes.

"And be so kind, private, tell me what's the matter. Is something bothering you?"

"Yes, I…"

"Get up first."

Ginger slowly got up and stood with his back to the wall.

"I'm bothered by the fact that our radios aren't charged."

The Sergeant nodded his head.

"And you should have checked it," Ginger concluded.

"I heard you," the Sergeant replied. "You can write a report to the commanding officer about this fact. Are there any other questions?"

"Not right now."

"Then go and check the signals and tripwires."

Damn him, the Sergeant thought, following Ginger with his gaze. *What's up with him?*

Who called him Ginger, anyway? he tried to recall – and suddenly he did.

It wasn't anything special: back in distant Russia, they were sitting around and drinking, and that guy was sitting to the side – he had recently joined the unit.

"What are you sitting there for the whole time, on the side?" the main unit's joker asked, the deputy engineering specialist, who was thin and talked in a slightly nasal voice, and was nicknamed Sinew. "Why are you acting like a redhead?"

This wasn't funny in itself, but applied to the shining, hairless head it seemed amusing. Everyone laughed drunkenly.

"Aren't you sharp," Ginger had replied quietly. "That's a sharp tongue you've got there. You want to sharpen my pencil for me?"

"I won't sharpen your pencil, I'll jerk you off," Sinew replied, and everyone once more merrily bared their drunken fangs and pink tongues.

"All right, Ginger, don't honk," Sinew honked himself, quite amiably. "Come on, let's drink to brotherhood, to your new name."

For all his cheerfulness, he was brutal, Sinew was, and he was good at shooting people down, and liked to do so.

So that's how it came about: Ginger…

"What's with him?" Samara asked the Sergeant cheerfully.

"Go with him," the Sergeant replied, quickly calming down. "Or he'll fall over the tripwire. Make sure that…"

Samara, grinning cheerfully, went outside.

"Take an automatic weapon, where are you going with that oar of yours!" the Sergeant shouted after him.

Samara came back and put the sniper rifle in the corner, and took an AK-47.

"What's going on here?" Sluggish appeared.

The Sergeant shrugged his shoulders.

"Everything's fine, Sluggish," he replied, smiling. "Or shouldn't I call you Sluggish anymore?"

"No, call me Swift," he chuckled in reply.

Another dreary, limping hour dragged by.

Ginger came back and sat down in silence, staring ahead.

The others walked around him, as if he were not alive.

"Sergeant!" Sluggish called. "Could I have a word with you?"

"You hear what he's saying?" Sluggish nodded towards Vitka, when the Sergeant came over.

The Sergeant shook his head.

"He heard shooting at night. In the area of the village."

The Sergeant shifted his eyes towards Vitka.

"Not for long, just two minutes or so," Vitka answered quickly. "Even just a minute, probably."

"Who were you on duty with?" the Sergeant asked. "With Samara? Why didn't he hear anything? Was he asleep?"

Samara had already appeared behind him with a guilty look.

"Sergeant, I swear to you: I wasn't asleep. I just dozed off for a minute. Vitka shook me when the shooting started."

"Why didn't you wake me up?"

"It stopped immediately."

The Sergeant stood for a while, looking into the gun slit, with the wind blowing into his face… and he went outside, beyond the post.

He thought for a while, trampling a rock under his foot.

What should we do? Leave the post, go to the base?... No.

Send one person to the base on their own, or two people, to find out what's going on? Who? Sluggish and… Vitka. Yes.

Or should we all go at once? And leave the post? Who needs it… No, that's not right…

He turned around to enter the post, and suddenly in the distance there was a distinct rumble, as if an enormous sheet of canvas had been torn, and a land slide had begun. There was a dull thud and a resounding echo from the ground.

Samara and Vitya darted out of the post together, as though running from a fire.

They stopped still, because there was nowhere to run.

Everyone looked in the direction of the base: the racket was coming from there.

"We're being stormed, guys," the Sergeant said, not really recognizing his own voice, which sounded unusual.

"They're being stormed," Ridge said. He had also come outside, with the grenade launcher over his shoulder. "We're not, not yet."

"And we're not going to be," the Sergeant replied, and immediately raised his voice. "Right then, fuck it all, back into the post, quick."

For several minutes they clearly heard the sound of battle.

"Get ready," the Sergeant ordered. "Take the cartridge containers. Grenades, as many as you can. We're going to the base."

Everyone but Ginger started fastening combat vests, tightening bootlaces and collecting grenades – they were kept in two green crates at the post.

"What about the post?" Ginger asked.

"Get ready, private," the Sergeant said. "We're leaving the post. That's my decision."

The Sergeant took a pair of binoculars, and for a minute he surveyed the area around the post, first from one gun slit, then from another.

"Right, let's go."

At a quick trot, they made the run to a sparse grove which stood one hundred meters away from the post.

"Stop," the Sergeant commanded.

They all squatted on the withered grass.

"A car… Cars are coming," Sluggish said, looking at the road. "From the direction of the base…"

The Sergeant heard the noise of motors himself even earlier. He also looked at the road, seeing out of the corner of his eye that Ginger was smiling.

He's probably happy that I'm going to get a dressing down for leaving the post, the Sergeant thought lazily.

"It's ours! It's our jeep," Sluggish stretched his pigmented cheek into a smile. "Let's go, what are we…"

"Stay there," the Sergeant said quietly.

The jeep drove almost right up to the post, with the front facing the entrance, and beeped: two, three signals in a row.

Sluggish stood up straight, looking in surprise at the Sergeant, and immediately squatted down again: out of the jeep jumped two bearded men, in a strange, bright uniform, and hid by the entrance to the post. Then another one jumped out, and crouching down, he jumped over to the gun slit, and seemed to take out a grenade of a sling, which looked expensive, and not Russian.

"Fuck me," Sluggish sighed. "Who are they?... They're Chechens. In our jeep. Shall we waste them?

Samara snapped his jaw.

Ginger clutched his automatic weapon, alternately grasping the grip and opening his palm: on the black metal a wet trace remained.

The grenade exploded inside the post: the bearded man had thrown it in. He threw another. And a third: it seemed to roll into the gun slit from the other side.

Following the car, another two jumped out, and they all crawled into the post.

They were absent for one and a half minutes.

"Let's go," the Sergeant said.

"Let's shoot them," Sluggish suggested, almost quivering with desire.

"We won't do it, you got that, Sluggish? We won't!" the Sergeant replied, almost growling.

"Why not?" Sluggish asked, and his nostrils quivered.

"Because shooting at a post is a waste of time. You can shoot for days on end. Or do you want to take it by storm? All six of us?"

"What about the car?" Sluggish asked scornfully.

"And what if our guys are there? Even one? Tied up? Do you want to shoot him?"

Sluggish moved his jaws, as if he wanted to bite something that prevented him from breathing, thrown on like a bridle.

Everyone looked, transfixed, at the post.

The bearded men came out, sullen and swift: they climbed into the car and sped off, back towards the base.

After a short distance, by the sharp turn-off behind the hill, which took them out of the line of fire, they fired a long volley at the grove.

Samara cursed so much that he almost fell on his stomach, Sluggish sank to one knee, and the Sergeant didn't move a muscle. The bullets went high: at the treetops.

They've guessed that we're here somewhere... the Sergeant thought. *And they're afraid themselves.*

"We should have met them at the post," Sluggish said. "I would have met them."

"You'd be lying there now with a hole in your head," the Sergeant replied, and went on ahead, into the thick of the trees.

Thirty seconds later he turned around: everyone was following him. He increased his pace, running. He heard breathing and the stomping of heavy men's legs.

If they took the short cut, they could reach the base at the same time as the jeep. The road for the jeep was much longer.

Shooting continued from the base, breaking off occasionally, and at these moments they stopped and caught their breath.

Ginger was breathing heaviest of all: he was carrying the case with the shells.

Never mind, let him... the Sergeant thought, but at the next stop Samara took the case.

Samara can take it then, the Sergeant agreed.

Two kilometers from the base, they walked more slowly, unhurriedly.

Soon our own tripwires will start, the Sergeant thought. *After all, I haven't seen them from this side... And they were put here by another platoon. Now we'll disturb our own grenade, that will be great...*

"Let's bear right, toward the road," he said after ten minutes.

Sluggish almost ran into his head: he was walking as stubbornly as if he had picked up a trail and didn't intend to leave his prey.

"What for?" Sluggish asked.

"Because," the Sergeant replied.

Shots were ringing out extremely close nearby, and this was quite terrifying.

Now, right now, they were about to run into people who wanted to kill them, and they would have to kill these people.

The soldiers looked around constantly.

They were mainly shooting from the base, in fact, the Sergeant thought, sitting down when the shooting got particularly persistent. And they were shooting high into the air.

"Sergeant, why aren't you saying anything?" the embittered Sluggish persisted.

"It seems to me that they're only shooting from our side," the Sergeant said.

Sluggish listened.

"So what?" he asked.

"It means they're shooting to frighten us rather than exchanging gunfire. Perhaps over there, in the forest, there aren't any Chechens. And the closer we get to the base…" the Sergeant breathed in some air, which was constantly in short supply – "the more chances we have… to get shot by our own people. You understand? And we're also about to run into our own tripwires. We could be blown up by them," he explained it all as if to a child.

Sluggish looked at him with mistrust.

"So what?" Sluggish asked again.

"Observe, observe, guys," the Sergeant said to the soldiers looking at them. "Or they might crawl out of somewhere…" and only then did he look at Sluggish. "We'll go towards the road. There are no tripwires by the road. And we can get a good look at the base from there. As long as they don't see us first."

They moved diagonally, away from the base: to the place where the road came through.

…The woodland came to an end, and open terrain began.

They squatted down, getting their breath back. They listened as the shooting started again. From here it was again unclear how they were shooting, who was shooting, and in what direction.

If only we had the radios… We're running around here… the Sergeant thought sadly, glancing sideways at Vitka, who seemed to understand the look, and turned away.

The Sergeant took out the binoculars and looked at the now visible road.

Our jeep probably drove past not long ago…

Now, if we can get to that left turn, the Sergeant realized – *then we will be able to see the base. We can see everything lying on the bank. But if someone drives past on the road… That will be stupid. There's nowhere to run.*

Two of us will go, the Sergeant decided. *With Sluggish? I'd take Ridge, but he has the grenade launcher. He'll be able to blow up any car from here… And Sluggish will instantly throw himself into an attack… I can't take Ginger. And I won't take Vitka either. And Samara is too young.*

"Let's go, Sluggish," he said. "Guys, cover us if necessary… Ridge, you're in charge. If you see a car with bearded guys stopping near us – shoot immediately. Aim well. Your shot will save us. If you hit them… And the rest can support you."

They could have crawled to the road, but this seemed completely humiliating.

So they ran, bending and grabbing the air with their clutching hands.

What idiocy, the Sergeant thought. *We're running like… Like idiots… We'll get to the road, and those bastards… will come to meet us… in their car… 'What's the hurry, soldiers?' they'll ask. And we'll turn around and run back…*

They made their way over the stones and ruts, almost breaking their legs... They ran across the road that they had driven along just yesterday, so free and calm, with their elbows out the window, and their sweaty faces grinning... There was the track from the wheels, dusty...

They slid down the bank on their backsides. They crawled to the turn.

Well then, base... How are you, base?... the Sergeant thought, listening. *We'll take a look, and see a black flag hanging there...*

What's going on in my country, he thought fleetingly. *Why am I crawling across it... not walking...*

There was the base. It stood at an angle to them. Two gloomy floors, and sacks over the windows. Nothing could be seen. No one was storming it, at least. There weren't any ladders against the building, no one was climbing in.

The Sergeant looked for a long time, squinting, and stupidly hoping that he would see someone's arm waving from the gun slit, or even a face, and everything would immediately become clear.

Then he took the binoculars, and pressed his face into them.

The base was impenetrable.

"What's going on there?" Sluggish said, unable to wait.

"Nothing," the Sergeant replied, and gave the binoculars to Sluggish: he wouldn't have believed anyway that there was nothing there.

Sluggish looked for a long time, and the Sergeant began to get tired of this: they should be returning to the wood, and thinking what to do next.

He felt thirsty.

He took out his flask and had a gulp.

Sluggish crawled off somewhere. The Sergeant looked after him sullenly, not calling out.

Pouring dust over his black beret, Sluggish raised himself up high, but did not look at the base, but somewhere to the side.

Again, the angry firing began – they were shooting from another side of the base that they could not see. From this side, there was nothing to shoot at anyway, apart from the road and the trees. From the base to the woodland there were three hundred meters of empty land and sand, and this was all in the line of fire.

But from the other side of the base, there were hills and some abandoned buildings, stables or cattle sheds. There were places where the bearded men could hide.

"I can see the jeep," Sluggish said, returning: his face was dirty, but dry, not sweaty – the Sergeant was surprised by this.

"Where?"

"Sticking out behind those buildings. They must have taken a detour to get here. Around the base. They didn't take this road. So our guys wouldn't shoot at them."

On the one hand, we need the jeep: it has a radio, the Sergeant thought. *On the other hand, the bearded men already have our walkie-talkies... And they know the wavelength. After all, they disarmed the guys who were coming to relieve us... Or killed them already... Let's not think about that, no need. No one was killed. Everyone's alive... What was I thinking about?*

"Sluggish, why do we need that jeep?" the Sergeant asked aloud, to avoid thinking.

"You don't need any fucking thing at all," Sluggish replied, licking white dust off his lips.

"I don't. You do. That's why I'm asking you: why?"

"It has the radio."

"I've already thought of that. The Chechens are probably using it already, on our wavelength. What are we going to say to that radio: *hello, brothers, we're in the woods? Someone come and get us!*"

"Is it better to sit here in the dust?" Sluggish asked. "Without any food?"

The Sergeant was silent briefly.

"Let's go into the wood," he said. "And in the evening, we'll go to the buildings. When it gets dark."

The Sergeant lay on the grass.

His whole body languished and ached from the inescapable feeling that there were other human animals in this forest, and that they could come here.

But there was nowhere to hide.

And nothing to think about.

Because any thought led to the fact that they could be killed today…

This was all so… stupid. As it turned out, that was the only way everything looked – stupid: at a time when something was reaching out for his very throat.

The Sergeant remembered how he had called his mother when he came here. His mother didn't even know that he was here: he didn't tell her when he left, he deceived her. And here he heard her voice in the receiver:

"I'll kill you, son, what are you doing!" she said.

The Sergeant even smiled: her words sounded so foolish, so good-natured, and therefore even more pitiful.

His mother herself was scared by her own *I'll kill you*: it was quite a common word at home, that was often uttered in a fit of temper, when as a child he broke something, or got up to mischief. But now this word took on a new meaning, terrifying to his mother.

I won't kill, don't kill, don't kill! she probably wanted to shout into the phone.

But there was no reason for this shout: on the second day after the unit arrived, they had their first and last normal shoot-out with the other side. Some bastards fired a few clips at the post and crawled back to their holes.

And that was all... Until today nothing serious has happened, mother.

You're still thinking about your mother, the Sergeant caught himself out.

I'm not thinking, I'm not thinking, I don't remember anyone, I don't remember my nearest and dearest, he waved aside these thoughts, realizing that if he remembered his other blood, poured into the world in the two pink, small, boyish, chick-like bodies, then he would go mad immediately.

I don't want to remember, I don't want to suffer, I want to eat rocks, I want to spin my stupid nerves into bundles, and I don't want to have to dream anything. I want to dream of stones, animals, primitive things...

Before Christ – what was before Christ: that's what I need. When there was no pity and fear. And no love. And no humiliation…

The Sergeant looked for something to lean on, but couldn't find anything: everything was weak and dragged you with itself to die, everything was full of soul, warmth and such tenderness that is intolerable for existence.

From somewhere, a sullen face summoned by his entire being came drifting along, it was stern, distinct and alien to everything that flowed inside. The Sergeant felt with his skull this inhuman, soul-strengthening glance…

He shuddered, and realized that he had fallen asleep for a second. Perhaps for even less than a second. And he had had a dream.

He squatted, looking into the semi-darkness.

"What did you see?" Samara asked.

"Stalin," the Sergeant replied hoarsely, thinking his own thoughts.

"Sergeant!" Samara exclaimed.

"Mmm."

"What's with you?"

"Everything's fine. Gather the posts. Let's go hunting."

They walked in the darkness, hardly concealing themselves.

The Sergeant said nothing to anyone. So as not to persuade them. And in any case he didn't want to talk anymore.

This is a foreign land, the Sergeant repeated, as if in a delirium. *A foreign land. Why does it want me so much?*

I used to be light… I felt light… I knew how to live lighter than snow… Why has it oppressed me so?

The land is breaking up. The crazy and trampled East. Apparitions, and the flickering remains of the West. And magma that will swallow everything.

…And there's nothing to hold on to..

"Where are you leading us?" Ginger asked.

The Sergeant kept silent, not at all comprehending what these words meant.

"I am leading you," he replied with difficulty.

"I don't get it, Sergeant," Ginger answered rudely. "I don't believe you, Sergeant. Where are you going?"

I also love my Homeland, the Sergeant thought, looking into the darkness and stumbling. *I love my land terribly. I love it horribly and immorally, not regretting anything… Humiliating myself and others… But what is spreading out under my feet – is that my land? My Homeland? What have you done with it, you…*

The Sergeant took out his flask, and drank the last gulp of water.

"Sergeant, why aren't you saying anything?" Samara asked, and his voice trembled.

And Vitka snorted nearby, looking the Sergeant in the face.

Only Ridge stood at a distance, confident and firm.

"What are you driveling about, everything's OK," Sluggish replied.

"Everything's OK," the Sergeant repeated loudly.

"You do remember where to go?" Sluggish asked him.

"Yes."

He remembered, and took his men through the darkness right to the buildings: one hundred meters from them, the soldiers squatted down.

Shots came from the base from time to time. Occasional flares cut through the darkness and hit the roofs and walls of the buildings.

A volley of automatic gunfire responded from somewhere nearby, and the soldiers thought that they were being shot at, they all immediately fell down into the sand, with their hands, bellies and faces… but the shots were being fired in a different direction.

"The jeep is parked there," the Sergeant said. "We're going to take it now."

"What for?" Ginger asked.

"We're going home," the Sergeant replied. "I'll take you home, Ginger," the Sergeant repeated angrily.

They crawled, stopping and listening from time to time.

The Sergeant licked salt off a stone and ran the crunchy grains of sand over his tongue and lips.

He did not have a single thought in his head.

"…there's no key there…if…there's no key?" the words reached him: Sluggish was whispering.

"I'll start it," the Sergeant replied. "I'll take off the hood… cables… I can do it… Shit."

Twenty meters away they lay down and stayed there for a few minutes, without moving.

Someone laughed inside the buildings.

And it was quiet again.

"Ridge," the Sergeant called. "Everyone will get into the car, and you get in the back, in the box."

The "box" was what they called the section behind the seats in the jeep.

"When I start moving, shoot from the grenade launcher… at them."

Ridge nodded.

"Wait," the Sergeant said to everyone and crawled ahead.

Slowly, slower than a blossoming flower, he crawled the last meters to the car. He lay by the wheel, stroking the tyre, as if the iron jeep was an animal that could be scared.

The Sergeant got up, and bending over, trying to tread quietly, walked around the car.

He searched for the handle… there it was, ice-cold… He raised his head and looked in the window, expecting to see crazy eyes stuck to the glass from the other side. There was no one there, no eyes.

He pushed the handle down and pulled the door towards him.

He stuck his head inside, and smelled rather than looked. It didn't smell of a living, sleeping person.

It smelt of the strangers who had left, dirt, sweat and gunpowder.

The Sergeant put his leg in, and then moved his entire body into the car. He stretched out on the seat and even shut his eyes for a second.

Don't think, he begged himself.

He felt in the dark car with his blind hand and shuddered: it seemed to be the key.

He bent over: yes, the key. In the ignition. They hadn't taken it.

Why the hell should they take the key, who would steal the car here…

And the radio… Where's the radio? There it is.

There was laughter in the buildings again: ridiculous, foolish laughter.

The Sergeant listened, and suddenly thought quickly: *They're out of it… That's how people laugh when they're out of it… They probably looted the pharmacy in the village…*

He felt light, light and clear, and everything fell into its place.

He touched the steering wheel, the gear stick, the pedals, adjusting to the car, so that he wouldn't get anything wrong.

And no one's storming the base, he thought, not hurrying himself. *They blocked it. They're waiting for their own guys, I suppose. Reinforcements. Our guys are probably all fine. There wasn't any assault on the base. Good. Look alive, men. The planes will be here soon. And those bastards will get it… they will…*

The Sergeant bent over across the seat and opened the door on the right.

"Sluggish!" he called quietly.

Sluggish climbed into the car calmly, as if he was stealing it from his father's garage, and not…

"Don't slam the doors," he said to the others, when Vitka, Ginger and Samara climbed into the back.

"Fuck it, we've got to turn around," Sluggish said. "Can you?"

"Is Ridge there?" the Sergeant asked instead of replying.

"Yes," Sluggish sighed, turning around.

"Let's go," the Sergeant said, turned the key, and switched on the headlights.

In the blinding beams of the headlights, 30 meters away, a bearded man was standing, swaying, with an automatic weapon over his shoulder, and urinating on the wall of the building. It seemed as if the light had caused him to sway. He turned his head, not at all surprised.

For a fraction of a second everyone looked at him from the car. The Sergeant was already starting the engine.

"Hey, who turned on the light? Are you nuts?" someone shouted inside the building, in a nasty voice, with an accent, but in Russian.

The engine started on the second try.

"For the Homeland," the Sergeant said, and moved into first gear. "For Stalin."

In second gear, he stepped on the gas and the man with the weapon went flying on to the bonnet of the car, before he had time to realize what was going on.

The Sergeant immediately put the car in reverse, knocking the limp body off the bonnet, and drove out onto the square in front of the cattle barn.

Furiously turning the steering wheel, he turned around and drove off, not seeing the road to start with – jolting, risking stalling every second – and then suddenly, by intuition, he drove on to it.

Fourth gear… They flew along, yelling and weeping.

Something flared in the car, and instantly rose and blazed in the rear-vision mirror.

"Great, Ridge!" the Sergeant yelled, guessing that Ridge had fired the grenade launcher. "Waste them, Ridge!"

Sluggish, turning around and pushing his legs into the seat, shot from the automatic weapon, putting it out the window and not taking his hand off the trigger.

"Sluggish, asshole!" the Sergeant howled. "Call our guys!"

"Base! Base!" Sluggish yelled, turning around and grabbing the radio. "Base, it's us! It's the Sergeant!"

They sped on and didn't hear shots behind them.

"Base, for God's sake!" Sluggish yelled.

"Receiving?" came a distant, questioning voice.

"It's us! In the jeep! Don't shoot! You understand? Base, for heaven's sake! Don't shoot!"

"Over," came the distrusting reply.

They sped up to the building and all fell out together, in a single moment.

The Sergeant painfully tore his hands away from the steering wheel: it cost him incredible effort.

The heavy door was opened for them: the Sergeant saw in the glare of the headlights that heavy bags were being moved inside the building, freeing up the entrance.

Ginger ran in first, then Samara, then Vitka.

Ridge moved his body inside.

Sluggish changed clips and shot into the darkness from his belt.

"Come on, Sluggish, let's go home!" the Sergeant said to him.

Scowling, he jumped into the darkness of the building, and the Sergeant took a step after him.

He was thrown back heavily and slowly, exploding somewhere in the air. But then he unexpectedly stood lightly on his feet and made a few very gentle, almost weightless steps, coming out of the line of fire. Somewhere here, his own men should be waiting for him, but for some reason the Sergeant did not see any of them, but for all that he did feel with all his being the good, almost sweet semi-darkness.

Damn, how am I… how did this happen to me? the Sergeant said, surprised at his luck, and turned around.

The black, evil smoke dispersed, moved away and disappeared, and he saw a person with his arms and legs splayed clumsily, and his head thrown back: one eye was black, and the other was shut.

CPSIA information can be obtained at www.ICGtesting.com
Printed in the USA
LVOW010854151212

311738LV00009B/478/P